THE CUBE PEOPLE

Nightwood Editions • 2010 • Gibsons, BC

The
CUBE
PEOPLE

A Novel

Christian McPherson

Nightwood Editions
P.O. Box 1779
Gibsons, BC V0N 1V0
Canada
www.nightwoodeditions.com

THE CANADA COUNCIL | LE CONSEIL DES ARTS
FOR THE ARTS | DU CANADA
SINCE 1957 | DEPUIS 1957

BRITISH
COLUMBIA
ARTS COUNCIL
Supported by the Province of British Columbia

TYPESETTING: Carleton Wilson

Nightwood Editions acknowledges financial support from the Government of Canada through the Canada Book Fund and the Canada Council for the Arts, and from the Province of British Columbia through the British Columbia Arts Council and the Book Publisher's Tax Credit.

This book has been produced on 100% post-consumer recycled, ancient-forest-free paper, processed chlorine-free and printed with vegetable-based dyes.

Printed and bound in Canada

LIBRARY AND ARCHIVES CANADA CATALOGUING IN PUBLICATION

McPherson, Christian
    The cube people / Christian McPherson.

ISBN 978-0-88971-251-5

    I. Title.

PS8625.P53C83 2010   C813'.6   C2010-904331-6

for Molly and Henry
my world, my gravity

The Cube People

Fertility

I'm waiting to masturbate into a cup. I realize fairly quickly that not everyone here is waiting to do the same thing. A chubby elderly woman sits three seats down reading *Cosmopolitan*. She's wearing grey sweatpants and a white T-shirt with an orange smiling-sun cartoon poking out from behind the words "Orlando, Florida." Her left leg is extended and her foot is wrapped in a tensor bandage. Crutches lie in the seat beside her. Her breasts are big and droopy and they hang down to her stomach like a basset hound's ears. I try not to think about them, but then I involuntary flash to my grandmother's breasts, wilted watermelons dangling down to her navel. No, no, no, no. I close my eyes and rub my temples.

"You okay?" asks a female voice.

I sit up and open my eyes.

"You okay?" repeats a semi-attractive lady across the aisle.

"Ahhh, yeah, no, just a bit of a headache is all," I tell her. I note that she's extremely pregnant. She looks like she swallowed one of those giant exercise balls.

"Yeah, I get those all the time," she tells me, her concerned face turning into a smile.

"Ah," I say, not really wanting to talk.

My wife and I have been trying to get pregnant for over a year now. We recently went to a fertility specialist, Dr. King. He thinks he knows what the problem might be – PCOS, Polycystic Ovary Syndrome. However, he said he wanted to cover all the bases, so he sent me for a test to make sure my sperm is good, too.

I'm worried that I won't be able to perform. I want to stay focused on the task at hand, the task that will literally be in my hand quite soon. God, pregnant women and grandma titties, I definitely need some better fodder for my fantasy love tug. I think about my wife's breasts. I think about my ex-girlfriend's breasts. I think about the breasts of the girl I saw standing at the bus stop on my way here. The pregnant lady is still smiling at me, waiting for me to engage her in conversation.

"How far along are you?" I ask politely.

"My due date was yesterday, so I think I'm going to have to be induced if he doesn't show up soon. I had to be induced for my first, I was ten days late. Are you here for sperm analysis?"

I feel my face flush. Christ almighty – am I here for sperm analysis? You have to be kidding me. I contemplate asking her if she's planning to give up the baby for adoption. Isn't there any privacy anymore?

"Yes, I am."

"My husband had to do it, too. Nothing to be embarrassed about, I'm a nurse. I just took an educated guess, after all, this is a fertility office. That's what all men come in here for usually."

Just as she finishes saying that, I see a guy about my age appear from around a wall. He looks a little dazed, bewildered, spent. He quickly glances around the room, then dashes for the front door. A short chubby nurse, with a clipboard and a plastic cup in her hands, comes around the counter and says, "Colin MacDonald?" I stand up waving my hand. The pregnant woman across the aisle whispers "Good luck," as if I were about to perform for an audition or head in for a job interview.

Good luck on what, getting an erection? Fear grips me again. As I follow the nurse down the hall, I try to think sexy thoughts. But all I can do is watch the white fabric of the nurse's pants being devoured by the hungry crack of her stop-sign-wide bum. I try not to look. I try to think of what nurses look like in pornos – white thigh-high stockings, short miniskirts, tight shirts with boobs about to pop out, and little caps with the red cross on the front.

The nurse leads me down a narrow hallway to a window-less room the size of a walk-in closet with a minuscule ensuite bathroom. A plump armchair takes up almost the entire width of the room, a picture of a sailing ship hangs high on the wall, a small trolley sits next to the door, and a magazine rack is mounted on the wall. The nurse hands me the cup. "When you're done put the cap back on and mark your name and the time on the label. Place the sample in this warmer. Here in this rack are some magazines if you need any assistance. I recommend you lock the door. Any questions?"

"Umm, I guess not. Just put the sample in there?" I confirm, pointing down at the bottom of the cart to the little rectangular box that is emitting bubbling sounds similar to a fish tank.

"Right," she says closing the door behind her.

I lock the door.

My grade five teacher, Mrs. Dunbar, was a knockout. She had long dark hair and always wore snug turtlenecks and tight slacks. My buddy Gord and I had many recess debates about whether or not Mrs. Dunbar did it. I knew she was married because she wore a ring, but I still wasn't convinced that she really did it with Mr. Dunbar. Gord, on the other hand, was convinced. "I bet they go at it all the time," he would tell me.

As the school year progressed, Mrs. Dunbar suddenly took to wearing dresses. I hadn't really attributed anything to this shift in wardrobe. Then after three months of wearing this new attire, she came into class and dropped the bomb. She was pregnant. Then I had known for sure she did the nasty.

I think of Mrs. Dunbar as I unzip. My pants fall around my ankles. Looking to my right, I see the sailboat. I try to imagine Mrs. Dunbar in a bathing suit, sunning herself on the boat's deck. I pull my underwear down to my ankles and stare. Nothing. It just hangs there, pathetic, flaccid. I play with it a little and try to picture Mrs. Dunbar naked. I can feel some blood moving and life is springing into the monster, into Marvin. Yes, I too have named my appendage. Why Marvin? Actually I didn't name him, my wife did. Marvin the monster, who roams around in wet slimy caves. It seemed funny at the time.

Marvin is a tad sluggish. Tugging at him some more he plumps up a bit. I realize I can't do this standing up, so I shuffle backwards like a prisoner in ankle chains, toward the chair, and I'm just about to sit when I flash to all the dirty asses that have jerked off in that chair. Marvin shrinks back down. I shuffle to the bathroom and pull out a ream of paper towel. I bring it back to the chair and lay it out in two strips. I sit down. Yank yank yank on Marvin. Blood returns, but the horrific image of the fat nurse's butt ass-munching those pants is stuck in my head. God, why does my brain keep going to that? And this brings me back to the old lady's tits in the waiting room, the one with the crutches. This is a fertility office, so she isn't here about her leg, but rather to get a Pap smear or something – Oh God, Sasquatch bush. Must get rid of these visions. Time to invoke the porn. As I stand up, the paper towel sticks to my butt. I pull it off and scuttle the two feet to the magazine rack to grab the only issue there, *Penthouse: The International Magazine for Men*, Oct. 2003. The rag is old and there are pages missing. Some are stuck together. Gingerly I place it on the arm of the chair, trying not to touch it as much as possible. It flops open to a page where the caption reads, "Diving her tongue deep into the beautiful blonde's honey pot." Marvin responds well to this. I readjust the paper and sit back down. Still, it doesn't completely quiet my mind – fat-ass crack-munching pants keep popping up.

"No!" I yell, and then realize that maybe the nursing staff or the people in the waiting room might be able to hear me.

I think of all the other guys who have been through this madness. There must have been thousands of men in here before me, trying to think of all kinds of weird sexual stuff, trying not to think of their grandmothers' tits. That's what gets me going, not the guys masturbating before me, but their fantasies. I think of the girl-on-girl action, the honey pots, the whips, the chains, the group sex, asses, nipples, vibrators on full throttle. My mind is a swirling vortex. Ass fuck, cucumbers, chickens, anal wands, whipped cream, blindfolds, vaginal piercings, the girl at the bus stop, Britney Spears videos, Sarah's mouth moaning, Mrs. Dunbar biting a pillow. A tornado! And there's the Wicked Witch of the West on her broom stick, except she's naked, and she's rubbing herself against the broom, sliding back and forth, back and forth. Bad witch, ohhhh, bad bad bad witch. Ohhhhhh!!!!!! BAD WITCH! BAD WITCH!! I fumble for the cup, get the lid off just in time as Marvin throws up. I look at my cellphone and note the time: 8:41 a.m.

I clean up my paper and write my name and time on the cup. I inspect my sample. Is it big enough? Am I producing enough sperm for Sarah? Maybe I've been choking the life out of my testicles with my boxer briefs. Maybe I should just wear plain old boxers? I use a tissue to grab the sample of the other guy who was before me and compare. I'm at least double. I note the name, Jerry Thompson. Jerry has hardly any sperm. I put the samples back and feel better that at least I have more juice than pitiful Jerry has.

I move out into the empty hall and shut the door behind me. I walk toward the waiting room. I glance and see another man about my age sitting there. I don't make eye contact with anyone, just dash out the front door. Now I have to catch a bus to work.

The Cube

I hate my job.

My government-laminated ID card dangles around my neck, bouncing and bobbing against my chest as I walk toward the scrutinizing eyes of the security guard. I pass by him and wait silently for the elevator with other bureaucrats. When I get to my floor, the air changes. It's recycled air, like on a jumbo jet. Something artificial about it. Unhealthy. I make my way through the rat maze of cubicles, listening to the soft clacking of keyboards, the sounds of scurrying insects as I go. When I get to the men's washroom, I'm there. My cube is next to the can.

I sit down on my black five-wheeled adjustable rolling chair with light-green fabric seat and backrest. I look to my right and see my Scooby Doo action figure sitting in the miniature blue foam sofa, a creative innovation of the stress ball that I picked up at a tech conference last week. Shaggy is positioned between Scoob's legs as if he were giving him head. I surmise this choreographed piece of plastic bestiality is the work of my co-worker and only real friend on the floor, Phil. At this I smile. Then I go about brewing myself an against-fire-regulations cup of coffee using my still while my machine boots up.

I work as a computer programmer for the Technology Branch of the Ministry of Revenue Collection (MRC), better known to most folks by its old-school name: The Tax Man.

I drink my coffee black. It matches my personality here at work. That's not entirely true. People like me. They think I'm good-natured and humorous. At least I think that's what they think. Who really knows? I don't give a rat's ass either way. Well maybe that's not really true either. I want people to like me. Sometimes I ramble.

COBOL is my bread and butter. It's an old programming language that most of MRC, the Ministry of Data Collection, and big banks run on. It stands for COmmon Business Oriented Language. It should really be CBOL, but COBOL sounds better. It almost seems as if they put that extra 'O' there just for me, a hole that sucks all of my time and energy, which has led me to my latest book idea.

More than anything I want to spend my days writing. So why don't I just quit and write? Bills, my friend, bills. I have a mortgage to pay and a beautiful wife. Why should she suffer for my writing career? Suffering for art is one thing, but making others suffer for your art is another. Besides, if you realized how much I hated my job, you would know I'm truly suffering for art. It's not the work I hate (I actually love coding); it's the environment. It's this cubicle land of government hell that I find myself in.

My cubicle is a quad. That means I share it with three other people. We all used to have our own workspaces until the Government Accommodations Initiative to maximize space and minimize spending was thrust upon us. It was sold to us as a

great way to foster a team environment. We moved from toler-
ance to our current state of being: we do our best to ignore one
another.

On my left sits Carla, a tall thin woman who has that emaci-
ated vegan look to her. She's completely obsessed with germs
– the female version of Howard Hughes. She usually comes
in shortly after I do, while I'm in the middle of my morning
email review. First thing she does is take a couple of hits off the
big bottle of hand sanitizer (the only item on her desk aside
from her computer) and rubs her hands together feverishly.
Then she retrieves a bottle of cleaner and a roll of paper towel
from her filing cabinet and gives her whole desk a hose down.
Finally she sits down, removes a bottle of water from her backpack, and has exactly three small sips before removing the dust
cover from her keyboard and turning on her machine. I have
been witness to this antibacterial ceremony every working day
for the last four years. I don't know where Carla lives, what she
does in her spare time, or if she lives with anyone. As I said, we
do our best to ignore one another.

Behind me sits Dan. I have no idea what Dan does except
show up here at the office (occasionally that is, when he isn't
incapacitated with some sort of mysterious illness) and talk in
explicit detail about the latest medical procedure some butcher
of a doctor has performed on his failing body. Recently it's
been his teeth. Sometime last week after Dan ate a tuna sandwich for breakfast, he proceeded to lift the side of his upper lip
exposing his gums and a green-onion-encrusted molar, the way
you would inspect a dog's teeth. He told me how they had to
put in a bridge. Needles, drilling, bleeding, pain – for forty-five
minutes I listened and inhaled the fumes of Clover Leaf. The
next day Dan called in sick.

Next to Dan and behind Carla sits the German feminist

revolutionary and chain-smoker, Brita. She's at war with everyone and everything. Her hair is cropped military/lesbian short and today she's wearing a tight, black, studded dog collar, green camouflage fatigue pants, black boots, and a baggy, grey sweatshirt. I'd say that she cusses like a truck driver, but I don't think that a drunken truck driver would cuss as much as Brita. If it weren't for the angry getup, Brita would actually be quite an attractive woman. However, I don't think she has any interest in men, or women for that matter. She pretty much hates everyone. Everyone is a sack of shit, according to Brita, and everyone needs to know that our lazy North American capitalist way of life is causing the poor of the world to suffer terribly, enslaving its children and killing our environment. I do believe that Brita cheered when the World Trade Center went down. She's the female version of Brad Pitt in *Fight Club*.

In terms of coding styles, Brita and Carla are pretty much on the same page. Carla's code is aseptic – every IF, END-IF and TO are all lined up, everything easy to read, very clean. Brita's code is sparse, raw, and as a result also very clean. Dan, on the other hand, well, his code works okay but it's often convoluted, hard to follow and generally a mess.

There are seven emails in my inbox. One from Operations telling me that one of my batch jobs abended last night – a fancy way of saying that one of the programs, for which I'm responsible, broke down. I note the program name and delete the email. There is an email about a fundraiser bake sale for our Christmas lunch, even though it's only July. I delete it. There is an email from management that the amount of photocopying on the floor is too high, and to please use the photocopier responsibly. I delete it. Tracey, a girl I used to work with who now works for the Ministry of National Safety, sent me a piece of chain mail: if I forward it to ten people my wish will come true in ten minutes. I delete it. Somebody I've never heard of is going to be Acting Director, replacing somebody else I've never heard of. I delete it. A friend has forwarded me an MPEG of something entitled "Monkey Balls," but I'm firewalled here at work, so I delete it. Finally, there is an email from Phil wondering if I can get away sometime this week and hit the Werner Herzog retrospective at the Bytowne Cinema; *Fitzcarraldo* is playing on Thursday. I write him back that I'll check with Sarah. I delete the email as Carla walks in.

Squirt, squirt goes the hand sanitizer.

Writing

As I've mentioned, I want to be a writer. Science fiction/horror, this is my genre. For over eight years now, I've been pounding away at the keys, even managing to get a few short stories published – well two exactly, and one poem in an online zine. Not much I know, but you have to start somewhere.

I've received some positive feedback from editors such as "Almost went with this one, but ultimately the round table voted against it," or "For what it's worth, some of the editors said it would make a great movie. Good luck with your writing." Can you call that positive? I cling to the tenuous.

Mostly my rejections have consisted of form letters differing only by logo: "Thanks for your interest in our press, but at this time our publishing schedule is full."

Last Christmas I finished writing my first novel, *The Cube People*, representing three years of work. The protagonist, Setrac Sed (that's Descartes spelled backwards – not genius, however I was having fun) awakens on a raft, floating down a river and lands on the banks of Cube City, not knowing who he is or how he got there.

The people of this idyllic society worship the Cube. The Cube is a supercomputer that keeps track of all atoms within the walls of Cube City. Hence, the Cube knows or can predict what is going to happen to everyone and everything within the city. The Cube can prevent all accidents, all crime and all illness. Each citizen has a micro-processing chip implanted in his head to help the Cube keep track of all potential thought patterns.

I built in a love story with Setrac Sed and a woman named Zia. It turns out that the Cube knew that Zia was going to start a revolution in the future, which would ultimately destroy itself and the city. The Cube found multiple revolutionary pathways amongst its people (my fancy sci-fi way of saying, if the revolution hadn't begun with Zia, then somebody else was going to lead the revolt; it was inevitable). The Cube's solution to stop the revolution from happening was to send in Setrac Sed, who turns out not to be a man, but an android built by the Cube. Analogous to God sending Jesus to save us, the Cube sends Setrac Sed. What the Cube can't predict is the Cube itself. That is to say, the Cube can't keep track of its own atoms, its own thought patterns. Therefore, the Cube wasn't able to foresee that Setrac Sed would fall in love with Zia. Thus, this leads Setrac to kill his father, the Cube. Oedipus – who doesn't dig Greek tragedy?

Yeah I know, a little geeky, but I am a computer programmer after all. I find determinism fascinating. Imagine if there were a super computer that could keep track of every atom in the known universe. If you believe that atoms and molecules behave in certain set ways, then in theory you could predict exactly how everything was going to unfold. That super computer could map out your entire life. It would know for example that on July 17, 2026 at 1:23 p.m., you would be thinking about getting yourself a chocolate or maple walnut ice-cream cone, the choice you would make, and what kind of cheeky banter you would make with the clerk as you paid.

So what? That's what my wife would say. Poor Sarah. She doesn't care for science fiction. Somehow, I've managed to get her to read everything I've written. I'm a horrible speller. Sarah is God when it comes to spelling. So I say, thank God.

Just a few months ago, I sent the first three chapters of *The Cube People* to eighteen different publishers. Sarah helped me address and organize all the envelopes. "After all the help I give you, you'd better give me a baby," is what she said after we'd dropped all the packages at the post office. Did I tell you she was wonderful?

I'm restless. I always have to be working on something, writing. I've begun a new novel entitled *Hungry Hole*. It's a horror story. I work on it when I can, which is mostly in the evening, though sometimes I write at work. I have a lot of down time at work. There seems to be a lot of people with a lot of down time at work: e-Bay shopping, blogging, planning their vacations. I write. I don't feel bad about it. I work hard when there's work to be done. Plus I'm fast, which probably contributes to my free time. I just don't have the motivation to be a "Peter Cann," our resident Tech-3 on the floor. He's the man you go to when you can't figure out a difficult computer problem. He knows our mainframe system inside out. He's been here for decades and always makes time for you. Visiting Peter's cubicle is always an experience because he also has a worldly knowledge of many things: art, history, philosophy, you name it, Peter Cann can tell you about it.

I have no passion for my work. Doing the kind of code maintenance that we do in my shop is strap-a-sponge-to-your-chin-to-collect-the-drool boring. Your brain leaks out of your ears. It's worse than watching *Nashville* in the crappy seats of the Mayfair Theatre with a drunk and raving Phil beside you extolling the virtues of Altman's cinematic genius. That reminds me, I need to email Phil back about Thursday's film. Sarah gave me the okay.

The phone rings here in my office. It's the clinic. They've lost my sample. I have to go back in tomorrow to give them another cup of my essence.

Hungry Hole

A Novel by Colin MacDonald

Chapter 1

Ryan managed to hit the goddamn beam, *again*, on his way down to the cellar.

"Fuck," said Ryan.

"You okay honey?" asked a snickering voice from the top of the stairs.

"Remind me to pad this stupid thing, or get my legs cut off at the knees," replied Ryan as he continued to descend, rubbing his forehead, into what Gillian called, "*The-Amityville-Horror*-serial-killer-pit-of-hell." Two bare light bulbs illuminated old wooden shelves, boxes marked "office" and "bedroom" and Gillian's hardly used exercise bike. The flaking white walls exposed the rust-coloured underbelly of foundation, like the skin of a scab-ridden burn victim. Hunched, Ryan staggered to the little room in the front of the house inhaling a funk of mould, century-old sewers, mushrooms, earth, paint cans and cardboard.

On his way back he didn't notice the small crack in the concrete floor. He tripped, managing to smash the last Mason jar of hot and spicy dills.

"Shit," said Ryan.

"You okay honey?" asked Gillian again, this time with an even deeper laugh.

"I'm fine, but I managed to lose the last of the hot and spicys. Sorry."

"It's okay, just grab some of the extra garlic ones, and get another bottle of wine."

As the Rolling Stones' "Gimme Shelter" became louder, so did the stoned giggles of Dean and Marsha. He envisioned Gillian dancing barefoot with her glass of wine being beautiful, entertaining, being her usual self. He looked down at the mess he'd made. A tiny stream of brine trickled toward the crack, pooled momentarily at its edge – surface tension holding for a second – then broke and dribbled into the earth.

He cleaned up and brought Gillian her pickles. Dean and Marsha attacked the jar like savages. Gillian sexually deep-throated her pickle causing everyone to laugh to the point of crying. The pot was good.

"You might get some pickle action tonight buddy," said Dean as he nudged Ryan. Gillian winked at Ryan. Ryan smiled back.

All of a sudden, loud barking could be heard coming from underneath the window at the side of the house. "What the hell is that?" Dean asked.

"That's Spike, our crazy neighbour's pitbull."

"Jesus, friggin' thing sounds possessed," laughed Dean. "What's it doing?"

"Whenever somebody walks by on the street, it runs up and down between the houses as if it was one of Satan's very own hounds. The little bastard actually managed to get out once and bit me on the ankle."

"Good lord," said Marsha, biting into a pickle.

"Why didn't you have the thing put down?" asked Dean.

"I told Bill, that's the neighbour, I told him, 'Bill, if that dog ever gets out and bites another person, I swear to God I'll get him put down.' Bill said that was fair enough."

Everyone sat stoned, listening to the dog growling and running up and down beside the house. "I don't see anyone walking by," commented Marsha.

In the basement, the crack opened a little more.

Duck Feather Press
PO Box 521
Toronto, ON
M5T 8A1

January 2, 2006

Re: Manuscript Submission

Dear Colin:

Thank you for sharing your manuscript, *The Cube People*, with us. Duck Feather Press unfortunately does not publish works of science fiction. We are only interested in works of literature.

Best of luck with your writing.

Sincerely,

Judy Miller
Editor, Duck Feather Press

Six months later…

Crazy Larry and Suzy Scratch

I'm doing coding review on one of Dan's programs. It's a mess. I don't think he even bothered to compile the damn thing. I fill in the last comment box, number 15, on our standard code walk-through 811 form about which areas of code need to be fixed. Shortly after, I find yet another coding error. Another form is needed. I look for one in my filing cabinet, but of course I'm out. Off to the photocopier. I wouldn't dare ask Carla to borrow a walkthrough form to copy – touching one of her pieces of paper might throw her into cardiac arrest. I'd ask Dan, but he called in sick again. Brita has her headphones on, her right leg is bobbing up and down, a piston, and I can make out the tinny sounds of heavy metal. Her headphones are big and make her look as if she might be running the radio on a World War II submarine. She appears to be reading some online leftist news service. I deduce this from the hammer and sickle in the upper left-hand corner of the screen. I tap her on the shoulder. She removes her headphones – screams and pounding drums erupt from the speakers. I'd have a headache within a minute.

"Yeah, what is it, MacDonald? What can I do you for?" she spits.

"Can you give me an 811 form to photocopy?"

"Yeah, yeah, shit, just a second," she huffs as she pauses her music.

"Don't want to miss a note of that," I say.

"Fuck MacDonald, you got something against Slipknot?"

"No no, I'm just kidding you, Brita. Just seems a little loud for me."

"We're living in the bondage of capitalism. What happens when you don't pay your taxes?"

"Umm, I don't know, maybe nothing. There are all kinds of things that could happen. We'd probably send you a letter asking you to please pay."

"But after, after you don't pay for a long time, do you know what happens MacDonald? You go to motherfucking jail. The cops show up at your house with guns and drag your ass to the slammer because you didn't pay your taxes. How can we call this freedom?"

"But you work for the MRC, you're one of the people responsible for putting tax dodgers in jail."

A strange look, a mix of confusion and anger washes over Brita's face. "Here's your form, MacDonald. Make sure to bring it back," she gruffs.

"Thanks," I say.

As I exit the quad, I hear Carla open her drawer. *Shhech shhech* goes the spray bottle. This is normal procedure after anybody exits our quad. Walking along the outer wall I see Crazy Larry, or at least that's what Phil and I call him. I'm not sure what group Larry works for, or what he does, but he's built himself a cardboard wall/barrier made from the green tops of paper boxes. Taped to the boxes is a handmade sign offering the following information: *I'm wearing earplugs. If you wish to contact me please send me an email. Thanks for your cooperation. –Larry Young.* If there were ever an employee to go postal it would be Larry. I often listen, waiting to hear the cocking sounds of a rifle. If I ever do hear a shot, I know which way I'm going to run. Once some movers dropped a filing cabinet – BOOM! – I shot out of my seat at warp speed. I was halfway down the hall, heart racing, palms wet, when I realized that Larry, nor anyone else for that matter, wasn't shooting.

He's standing up, as he often is when I walk by, looking out the window at the parking lot. I can see the yellow circle of the industrial earplug wedged in Larry's oversized melon of a head. His lips are moving ever so slightly but I can't make out anything he is saying. I wonder if he uses the same earplugs over and over, or does he use fresh ones daily, or maybe he changes them on a weekly basis?

Larry too is in a quad, but two places are empty. The only other occupant is Suzy Scratch, who sits diagonally across from Larry. From all accounts, Suzy is an old veteran, has been around MRC from the time they used punch cards. Apparently, she suffered some sort of collapse in the nineties and was off work for a while, but when she came back, she just wasn't the same. Every time I walk by, Suzy is busy scraping away at a scratch-and-win lotto ticket. She never seems to have any work to do; she's just waiting to hit it big I guess. I puzzle over what she'd do if she actually won. As I pass by the entrance to their quad, I glance back and sure enough, there's Suzy scratching away. I continue down the hall to the coffee room where the photocopier resides. A large notice has been placed on the wall above the copier:

```
Attention ALL STAFF: Photocopying is
at an all-time high. Please think
twice and copy once. Thanks for your
cooperation in this important matter.

-The Management
```

I look at the walkthrough form in my hand. "Do I really need to photocopy you?" I ask the paper. The paper doesn't reply and I grow incensed at its silence. I feed it into the machine and select a conservative ten copies rather than twenty. Peter Cann comes waltzing in with an empty coffee mug and heads over to the communal twenty-five-cents-a-cup pot and pours himself one. He sees me and says with a smirk, "Take it easy, photocopying is at an all-time high."

"I see that," I say as the copier spits out my last page.

"Hey, I finished off *The Cube People* last night. I thought it was really really good. The analogy of art as freedom against determinism was really interesting."

"Hey Peter, wow, that's great. It means a lot that you liked it."

"I think you've got talent, Colin. You hear anything back from any publishers yet?"

"One rejection so far. I'm not optimistic."

"Don't be discouraged, it'll happen for you. Are you working on something now?"

"Yeah, a new novel called *Hungry Hole*."

Peter smiles at the title.

"More science fiction?" he asks.

"More horror than sci-fi."

"You know I tried to read Stephen King's *Pet Sematary* and threw it straight into the trash. Awful garbage. However, *The*

Dead Zone was one of the finest pieces of literature I've ever read. So I say to you Mr. MacDonald, keep it up," he says raising his cup in salutation as he leaves.

I feel good. I'd given him a copy of *The Cube People* because he'd asked to see it. I didn't actually expect him to read it, let alone like it. I can't wait to tell Sarah.

On my way back I notice that Larry is no longer staring out the window, and because I'm not looking straight ahead, I don't see Larry when he comes barrelling, head down, out of his quad. We crash into each other. This scares the bejeebers out of me and I nearly drop my paper. Larry's bug-eyed face is only inches from mine. "Sorry," I blurt out.

Larry doesn't say anything to this, doesn't apologize either. He just stares at me, confused. "I think they know," he blurts out, then continues down the hall.

"Fucking freak," I mutter to myself, passing Suzy, still hunched over her desk, scratching.

When I get back to my quad, I can smell disinfectant coming from Carla's desk. I glance over at Dan's desk and see a decaying, half-eaten muffin lying beside his keyboard. Is this some passive-aggressive move on Dan's part to drive Carla batty? Not his style – he's just a plain old slob.

"Here's your 811 back," I say to Brita, although I doubt she can hear me.

She swivels in her chair and responds loudly, likely due to Slipknot blasting in her ears, "Just put it on the fucking desk MacDonald, Jesus, can't you see I'm coding here?"

I log back onto my machine and an email from Phil greets me wanting to go to lunch; apparently he's starving and about to lose his mind. Before I even click reply, Phil appears at the entrance of my quad. He performs a huge fake sneeze in Carla's direction. Carla looks like somebody just told her that a family member had died.

"Must be coming down with something," says Phil.

I try not to laugh.

"You ready dude?" asks Phil.

"Yeah, let's go."

"Time to get the fuck out of Dodge, baby."

I lock up my machine, alt-ctrl-delete, as I hear Carla open her drawer for the spray.

Sunshine Valley Mall

I don't really know why Phil bothers to email me about lunch; he comes by my desk at the same time every day and says the same thing, "Time to get the fuck out of Dodge." Dodge, our office building, is located across the street from a shopping mall. If I don't bring my lunch, which Phil never does, this is where we go.

We frogger our way across the street through heavy traffic and into the temperature-controlled environment of Sunshine Valley Mall. Escalators carry us upwards through the suspended 3-D fibreglass clouds. When we reach the top, the bustling noise of hungry shoppers is almost deafening. A huge wrought-iron archway with the words "Sunshine Court" greets us. Choices abound. Neon and fluorescent lights illuminate the culinary repertoire of such fine eateries as New York Fries, Pizza Pizza, Subway, Tim Hortons, McDonald's, KFC and the family-run Lebanese place, The Shawarma Pit. We've been coming here for years and don't bother to discuss where we're going to eat. I hand Phil seven bucks and look for a good seat near the tranquil artificial rock mound, equipped with a soothing waterfall, goldfish pond and lush plastic plants. From this magical vantage point, we can gaze into the den of beauties, the all-female staff of First Choice Haircutters. Phil gets his haircut at least once a month, usually from Lulu, the clipper with the biggest breasts. Within five minutes, Phil has returned from The Shawarma Pit with a couple of waxed-paper-wrapped chicken sandwiches, garlic potatoes and sodas.

"Lulu there?" he asks, rubber necking to the hair salon as he sits down.

"Haven't seen her yet."

"Hey, is that one new?" he asks, referring to a young blonde woman with an almost indecently short, black miniskirt.

"Yeah, I think so. Looks pretty hot."

"Fucking right on. I need my haircut anyway. It's a friggin' mop."

"Phil, you hardly have a mop, it's a crewcut."

"Bullshit, I need a haircut. How's Sarah, you guys pregnant yet?"

"Sarah has PCOS and has been on this Metformin drug to help regulate her blood sugar. The idea is that she will start to ovulate normally. It's been six months now and still no luck. We're going back to see Dr. King next week to see what the next step is. Sarah's depressed. She keeps talking about adopting a little girl from China, but I keep trying to tell her to keep her hopes up and not give up. Adoption's bloody expensive. Over twenty grand if you want a kid from China and it takes three years."

"Holy shit," says Phil as he shovels a garlic-covered potato into his mouth.

"Yeah, crazy eh?"

"Fuck, do you at least get to pick the kid yourself, or is it random?"

"Pretty sure it's random."

"Christ, so you could get a real ugly one then?"

"Dude, that's not very nice. Sarah and I, if we ever do manage to have kids, well they just might be the ugliest kids in the world."

"You and Sarah, ugly kids, I don't think so. The only ugliness would be coming from you, so I think the kid would have a pretty good chance. Hey, look there, it's Freddy Fruitcake," says Phil, pointing to a man who's slowly walking down the mall carrying a flashlight.

Phil's coined the name "Freddy Fruitcake" only because Freddy is obviously mentally ill. Freddy snakes detective-like through the mall armed with a flashlight and attired in his standard uniform of neon green pants and orange baggy sweater. Freddy and the Sunshine Valley Mall were partially my inspiration for *The Cube People*. I always envisioned the cube, this supercomputer, to resemble this food court, a giant glowing brain with a beehive of drone workers, coming and going – happy cube people in their idealistic society, eating the same thing repeatedly.

"Phil, why do we eat at The Shawarma Pit almost every day?"

"Dude," he muffles, taking a swig of his drink and washing back the food, "the food is the bomb and the girl at the cash is smoking. But you know this already, so why are you asking? You're thinking about determinism again aren't you?"

"Maybe," I say, always amazed at how intuitive Phil can be.

"Shit man, I told you, it will unfold as it will, so you should focus on the here and now. If you sit around thinking about how it is you're thinking all the time, well life is just going to pass you by, man. Live it as if it means something and you will find happiness."

"Phil, have I told you recently that you're one awesome dude?"

"Shit man, I know that. Now I just have to convince the new little hottie at First Choice of that fact and life will be grand."

We finish our lunch and head to First Choice so Phil can make a hair appointment for 4:30. He flirts heavily with the new girl. When we get back to the office my project leader and immediate supervisor, Bruce, is exiting my quad. Bruce is a micro-manager, a nitpicker – typical red-tape government. I always feel compelled to tell him, just let me do my job for Christ's sake and quit all the nonsense. "Hey Colin, hate to be a pest, but can you resubmit your timesheet for last week, you used code 855 when it should be 856 for the two-hour meeting on Wednesday."

"Sure thing Bruce, right away."

"I'm going to have estimates for you soon."

"Sounds good."

"Oh yeah, I'm supposed to remind everyone that photo-copying should be held to a bare minimum. Also, try not to print anything if you can."

I think of Bruce as not responsible for his actions, like Freddy Fruitcake. They have no choice. Bruce can't help being Bruce. I correct my electronic timesheet and hit submit. I smile and think I can't help the fact that I hate my job.

Bacon Phat Editions
PO Box 4550
Fredericton, NB
E4B 7Q7

June 15, 2006

Dear Mr. MacDonald:

Thank you for your submission. Unfortunately, we are looking for titles that are edgier, riskier. *The Cube People* is just not alternative enough for us.

We have recycled your manuscript as you indicated was your preference in your letter.

Best of luck.

Sincerely,

Jim Phat

Hungry Hole

Chapter 2

A week later Ryan went back down to the basement to get out his bicycle for the first spring ride. The crack in the floor was now an indentation about the size of a basketball. It looked like part of the foundation had collapsed into the ground.

"Shit, look at that," said Ryan aloud.

He got down on his knees and felt the concrete to see if it was wet, to see if there was some sort of leak. It was their first house. They'd been living here just shy of a year. The home inspector had said that the people who'd built this house had built it to last. The roof, wiring, plumbing, foundation were all sound. Even still, during the first few months of home ownership, every time it rained, Ryan found himself in the attic checking for leaks and in the basement checking for flooding. After a while he'd stopped. Gillian was a calming influence. You worry too much, relax, she would tell him, it's all going to be okay. Relax, yeah right, look at this hole, thought Ryan.

Within an hour he was back from Home Depot with cement. He mixed it according to the clerk's instructions and then filled the hole.

Two blocks into the bike ride he noticed a construction site. A massive lot of expensive row houses were going up. Men in hardhats were working on the foundation. Ryan stopped his bicycle.

"Excuse me sir," said Ryan to a man wearing a white hat, whom Ryan assumed was the foreman.

"Yeah, what can I do for you?" asked the man, slightly adjusting his hat as he approached.

"Um, I just have a quick question for you, do you have a minute?"

"I'll try sir, but you'll have to make it quick."

"Well I bought a home just two blocks from here and a hole has formed in my basement floor."

"Uh huh," said the man, who didn't seem surprised at all.

"Well I just wanted to know if that kind of thing is common?"

"Well mister, let me tell you something, this whole area is built on clay. The houses around this area are slowly sinking. What we did with these houses is drop down titanium rods until we hit bedrock, a couple hundred feet. Now in your case, sounds like an air pocket, something way down probably shifted, up rises the air, down goes your floor. Still, not very common, but I've seen all sorts of crazy shit. Nothing much surprises me. Hopefully your whole house doesn't shift. If it does, you'll need my help. Here's my card," said the man, pulling one from his plaid jacket pocket.

"Thanks," said Ryan taking the card. "Hopefully I won't need to call."

The man smiled. "Yeah, 'cause it'll be expensive if you see me. Got to get back," he said and wandered back toward the construction site, yelling at another man to move some pipes to the other side of the house.

When Ryan came back from his ride, he studied the outside of his house from across the street. It looked straight to him. Inside the house he went over to one of Gillian's decorative glass vases and pulled out one of the dark blue marbles used to ground the artificial flowers in place. He placed it on the kitchen floor. Nothing. He rolled up the living room carpet and placed the marble there. Nothing. He went upstairs to the bathroom.

Nothing. The marble didn't roll. The house was, from what Ryan could tell, perfectly level. A slight sense of ease came over him. At least the house wasn't sinking. He descended into the basement to check how the cement was drying. As quickly as the ease had come, it left and was replaced with a sense of dread. The hole was back and bigger than before.

Bring on the Free Babies

Dan usually saunters in sometime between ten and noon. To-day he showed up at eleven and announced he would be leaving after lunch for a root canal.

"Jesus, Colin, the pain is unbelievable. I woke up last night around three and popped two Advils. It didn't take the bite off at all. Awful."

"Doesn't sound fun."

"God, you wouldn't believe it. Tell me, do I look swollen to you? Here on this side," he asks, swivelling his head back and forth so I can compare the size of his fatty jowls to one another.

"They look the same to me."

"Jesus, really, this side feels all swollen, like I've been stung by a bee or something."

"No, looks good. Hey, I have some questions about the change package you left in my in-basket the other day. You know, the changes you wanted me to make to Program 25."

"Oh yeah, did you finish it already?" he asks, massaging his apparently engorged cheek.

"No Dan, I haven't started it yet. I don't understand what you want me to do. It says to update the CT table, but that table is called from a different program."

"Oh, I just copied the specs. I guess I forgot to change the table name. It's pretty much the same as the other program, just add a few lines here and drop a few lines there. Not a big change. It shouldn't take very long at all."

"I don't care if it's big or little, I need to know what you're asking me to change. It's due on Friday."

"No reason to panic, Colin, I'll just give you the functional requirements and then you can understand what I'm talking about."

"Okay, let's get this straight, you want me to review the functional requirements, then fix the programmer's specs to match, right?"

"Well yeah, not a big change, it's pretty obvious when you're looking at it."

"But that's *your* job," I tell him. Dan looks hurt, as if I just told him to go fuck himself, which is really what I want to say.

"Gee whiz, Colin, it's not a big change. I'd do it right now, but I have to go across to the mall and pick up a prescription for my back before I go to the dentist. Everything hurts."

"I'll do it for you Dan," I mumble.

"Oh thanks, Colin. If you have any problems, just let me know and I'll be glad to help," he says smiling.

I know I should have more backbone when it comes to these kinds of things. The problem is if I wait for Dan to do it, it won't get done until after it's due, or just beforehand, if at all. I'll end up having to do it anyway. I don't need the stress. So I do it.

As I'm working the phone rings. It's Sarah. She'll be picking me up in thirty minutes for our fertility appointment with Dr. King. This will be our third appointment with him. My sperm results, by the way, were fantastic. I have nine times the motility of the average man. Queue the John Williams' *Superman* music please. A lot of people with PCOS tend to be big, fat. Some sort of insulin resistance. I don't really understand it completely, but basically it's very easy to gain weight. Sarah has large breasts, a bit of a gut, and a flat bum, but I wouldn't classify her as fat. Anyway, Dr. King suggested she lose a few pounds and prescribed her Metformin to help balance out the insulin sugar levels.

She's now lost ten pounds and has worked herself up from one Metformin pill a day to three, but she's still not ovulating. She's hoping that Dr. King will put her on some sort of fertility drug to get things moving, but she doesn't have a lot of hope these days. At night before bed she has been reading *The Lost Daughters of China*, a book about all the little girls being dropped off on doorsteps because of China's one child policy. There are thousands of little Chinese girls waiting to be adopted. Sarah thinks about them crying, wanting their mommy.

I go downstairs past the security guard and wait by the front entrance. When I see our desert-sand Corolla round the corner, I step out and wave. I get in. Sarah is crying. "What's wrong baby?"

"I just want to get pregnant," she blubbers.

"Well that's what we're working on baby."

"The Metformin gives me gas. I think this is fucking hopeless. Why don't we just get a girl from China?"

"Listen, babe, a girl from China is twenty thousand dollars. Making one of our own is free," I plead.

"I don't care about the goddamn money, I want a baby. I

want us to be a family."

"Right. Let's go see Dr. King and see what he has to say, okay?" I suggest as I softly stroke her shoulder.

Her bottom lip quivers and she wipes her eyes with a crumpled napkin from the glove compartment. "Okay," she agrees, driving away.

Dr. King's office is actually located at the Civic Campus of the Ottawa Hospital. In true hospital fashion, parking is limited, inconvenient and overpriced. You'd figure a place that catered to the sick and elderly would have a slightly more liberal parking philosophy. We corkscrew up to the top of a parking garage that has been under renovation forever. Six months ago they were working on it and they've made zero progress since that time. We walk down five flights of stairs, cross over to the adjacent building and take the elevator up to the sixth floor. We let the nurse know we're there and she tells us to take a seat down the hall. Today there is no one else in the waiting area. I look out the window and see our car parked on the roof of the next building.

A very pregnant lady waddles by. I watch Sarah's eyes lock onto her belly, as a cat would when it sees a mouse. Then I think about those women who are occasionally found splayed open like grade ten science frogs, their babies cut out. I imagine Sarah with her arm around the neck of the woman who just walked by, Sarah with some sort of Halloween knife in the other hand. Before I let the gruesome image go to where it is going, I give my head a shake.

Dr. King appears with his file folder. "Mr. and Mrs. Mac-Donald." We both stand up and follow him into his office. One wall is covered in thank-you cards with pictures of babies. He appears to have helped hundreds of patients, but he couldn't have been doing this all that long because he looks like Doogie Howser. He flips through Sarah's medical folder and looks at her recent blood tests. "So, still not ovulating, eh? Well okay then. We're going to try something else to get you to ovulate, Clomid."

Sarah smiles at this news and squeezes my knee. I can tell she's ecstatic. When I think of fertility drugs, I immediately think of twins, triplets, a full house. I imagine myself in a glass house where the public pays admission to see Sarah, me and our eight kids, the only way we can afford to feed all these babies. A wall of strangers' faces leering, pressed up against the glass, pointing and laughing as I run back and forth from one screaming child to the next. I give my head a shake. Different thoughts float in and out of my brain as Dr. King is talking. Twenty thousand is a lot of money to get a kid from China. I have a fear of flying. What did I do with the parking stub?

Sarah listens closely to Dr. King's explanation of how the drug works, its possible side effects, and when we should be having sex on the drug. Days 11 to 22 are the days we are to have, as Dr. King puts it, lots and lots of sex. "Try to do it every day, although every second day is good, too. Lots and lots of sex." I smile at this. Sarah removes her hand from my knee.

"How about twins, is there a high risk of twins on this drug?" I demand.

"Five to ten percent higher chance of having multiples."

I'm partially relieved to hear this, but I'm not completely satisfied. Maybe Ty Pennington and the design team from *Extreme Makeover Home Edition* TV show will come and rescue my ten-person family from the circus-freak-show glass house? "Multiple," I say aloud. The word comes out of my mouth like a burp, and I feel as if I should excuse myself.

"Twins would be okay," Sarah says. My eyes dart quickly back and forth between Dr. King and Sarah, waiting for him to say, actually twins would be awful, you don't want twins. However, nothing comes; they just stare back with inquisitive looks on their faces. Finally Dr. King asks, "You don't want twins, Colin, do you?"

"Uhhmm, no, I mean, I don't know, I guess so," I sputter.

"No worries, the odds are pretty low and you don't have any twins in either family, so it's not probable, but you never know. Try not to worry about it."

"Right, no worries," I say.

Dr. King gives Sarah a prescription for Clomid and goes over the dates again with her. He also gives her a requisition for a blood test to make sure that she isn't pregnant before she starts taking the drug, which is completely unnecessary, but he has to make sure. I guess he doesn't want to be sued for malpractice.

As we're leaving, Dr. King reminds us, "Days 11 to 22, lots and lots of sex."

Sarah clutches onto my arm as we walk back toward the elevator. "What do you think? Do you think it will work?" she asks.

"I don't know, baby, I hope so. We'll give it our best shot."

"If it doesn't work I want to get a little girl from China."

"Okay, don't you worry, Dr. King says he hasn't failed yet at getting someone pregnant that he believes he can. He believes in us."

"That's 'cause he's only twelve years old," Sarah jests.

I laugh.

We take the elevator down to the first floor and I sit in yet another waiting room while Sarah does her blood test. I flip through an issue of *Today's Parent* and wonder what kind of father I'll be. A smiling glossy baby in a diaper stares up at me from the pages. What if the kid doesn't love me? What if I don't love the kid? Well my old man is a drunk and he dumped my mother and me when I was ten and I still love him. I presume that I'll do better than he did – not much of a stretch.

Sarah appears. "I'm done, let's get lunch."

We get back to the car and Sarah suggests we head to Chinatown and hit our favourite spot, The Pineapple Thai Village. We arrive at half past one just as the lunch crowd is dying out.

We are seated two tables over from a white couple with a little Asian girl. Sarah spots them and her eyes well with tears. I place my hand on hers, smile and say, "We're going to have a family, one way or another. I promise."

She nods her head and tries not to cry.

My Night Out

I can smell hair products coming from Phil's head as we stand in line to buy tickets to a Hong Kong kung fu action picture at the Mayfair Theatre. Phil managed not only to get blond highlights, but Zoe's phone number as well; she's the new hot blonde from First Choice Hair Cutters in the mall. "One please," he says to the cashier. He turns to me and says, "Zoe and I are going out on Friday and I'm soooo going to get laid," then spins back around. Phil gets his ticket and change and bolts for the food counter. He meets me back in the lobby carrying a cardboard tray loaded with popcorn, sodas and a couple of bags of candy. Phil is always moving, always talking, animated. This is what makes him fun, but it can also be what drives people mad about him; he's on roller blades while the rest of us are walking. I wonder if Phil is actually manic-depressive? But I've never seen him depressed, just manic.

"Colin man, you should see the body on this girl, smoking. She's twenty-five," squeals Phil in delight. Phil's thirty-five, handsome, smart, has a good job – the ladies love him.

52

Strangely enough though, he's a bit of a geek. Or at least a movie geek. Maybe this is why he hangs out with me. I'm not really sure what he gets out of our relationship. Maybe I ground him a little. Anyway, for whatever reason, our brain chemistry clicks when we're together.

Before the film begins, Phil is particularly high, talking a mile a minute about Asian cinema, Zoe's breasts and legs, where he plans on taking her on Friday, Jackie Chan's childhood, why Nibs are the best candy ever, and an analysis of Tarantino's *Kill Bill*. I'm exhausted before the movie even begins.

After we watch what Phil described as "a fucking wicked martial arts film," we head to the pub next door for pints. I listen to him do his post-film critique for half an hour before the topic turns to having children. "I could have a baby with Zoe, man. Holy shit, would that kid be hot, I mean look at me," says Phil hoisting up his shirt, pointing out his six-pack abs. I'm not sure if Phil is entirely kidding; in fact I think he's serious, at least about the kid being hot. "But I could never be a father, I'm just too friggin' selfish," he blurts out with surprising honesty. "However you, my friend, will make a great dad. You have dad written all over you."

"Really, you think?"

"Shit man, you'll be fantastic."

"What if the kid doesn't like me?"

"You have the patience of a saint, you're warm and fuzzy, smart, shit, what kid wouldn't like you?"

"My stepsister's kid screams every time I go near her."

"Just a baby dude, they all fucking scream. Shit, women scream their whole lives. Don't worry about it."

"Yeah, I guess," I say as I sip my beer.

"Relax man, this whole baby thing has got you stressed out,

man. Have a few brews and chill. How's the new book coming along?"

"It's coming. I keep typing."

"Good man. Listen, it's going to happen for you, I can feel it. I'm not a big reader and I loved *The Cube People*."

"Yeah, that's what scares me."

"You're a funny guy MacDonald," Phil says, then turns his head around to the waitress who's wiping the table next to ours. "Can we get a couple more, darling?"

I stagger through my front door after fighting with the lock. My key always seems to stick after a few pints. I'm clutching a half-eaten shawarma. The light is on in the living room. Sarah's up. I sense trouble. "Where have you been?" she demands, flying out like a genie to the entrance in her pink nightgown, arms crossed.

"Out with Phil."

"Do you know what time it is?"

"Ah..." I say reaching for my cellphone but remembering that the battery died on me. "Ah, not sure, late?"

"It's a quarter to two."

"And?"

"You told me that you would be home at 12:30 at the latest. Why didn't you call? Christ, you stink of booze, how many pints did you have?"

"The phone died on me. I had four pints," I reply, lying about the number of pints.

"Why didn't you use Phil's phone or a payphone? Surely there's a payphone at the bar. Christ, how many pints did you really have?"

"Jesus Sarah, okay, relax, what's the big deal? I'm a little late.

The phone at the pub was out of order and Phil didn't have his phone on him. By the way, my name isn't Shirley or Christ," I say, chuckling at my own witty humour. I roll down the wax paper from my sandwich and take a big bite.

"That fucking stinks, Colin. You know the smell of that bothers me. You are so inconsiderate sometimes. You know I haven't been feeling well on the drugs, and you come in drunk, eating a fucking shawarma, and Christ, look!" she yells pointing at my feet. "You're dripping that shit all over my floor!"

Maybe it's the beer, maybe it's my belief that people are just victims of their own brain waves, but I don't bother to get mad. I just take another bite of my shawarma. Man, this is the best shawarma I've ever had.

"You're an asshole, Colin! Did you hear me? You're dripping the shit on the floor!?"

"Baby, relax, I'll clean it up."

"How many pints did you have? Tell me!"

"Okay, I had five pints," I tell her. I actually had six and a shot of Jagermeister.

"Five pints! Jesus Colin, Phil is turning you into some sort of alcoholic. I want to have a family. What kind of father are you going to be? You have to work tomorrow, for Christ's sake, or are you going to call in sick? You see Phil every damn day. Why do you need to be out with him until two in the morning?"

"I see you every day too," I say. I feel that my mind is sharp and clear despite all the booze.

"You're going to end up like your father!"

I've told Sarah many stories about Dad coming home liquored and fighting with Mom in the middle of the night. He'd punch holes in the walls, and in the morning he would inspect the damage. He'd tell me he was going to have to call the exterminator to get rid of the pesky woodpecker that was in the house. "That's over the top," I tell her.

"You're a fucking asshole. Go sleep on the couch in your precious writing study, 'cause you aren't sleeping next to me with that stinky mouth."

I'm getting tired of standing here in the hallway entrance getting yelled at. I think fine, time for bed. I take a step forward and slip in the shawarma garlic juice that has pooled on the floor. I stumble into the wall and knock a framed photo of Sarah's great-grandfather Gerald. I stand up, straighten the photo, and realize for the first time how enormous Gerald's handlebar moustache is. "Holy crap, that's a big moustache. Have you looked at this?"

Sarah's face is contorted with anger. "You can't even stand up!"

"Oh fuck off," I yell as I stumble to the study and slam the door behind me with all my might.

I wake up and it's still dark. I'm in a weird position on the couch where I presumably passed out. I've drooled all over one of the seat cushions. My shoes are still on. I really have to pee. I sit up. There's no light coming from underneath the door. Sarah must be in bed. Quietly I remove my shoes, trying not to wake her. The last thing I want right now is her screaming Janet Leigh style. Reaching to open the door, I realize the handle is gone.

We have a beautiful condo in Centretown. We're on the first floor of an old brick, three-storey walk-up. We have glass doorknobs. They're old, as is the building. About two months ago, the doorknob in here came loose. I hardly ever shut the door, except for the odd time when I'm trying to write and Sarah's watching TV. On the rare occasion when the doorknob falls off, I keep a screwdriver handy so I can pop the lock.

Now's the time I wished I'd called the maintenance man and asked him to fix it, because – although I have done it a half dozen times before – I can't for the life of me pop this darn lock. Shit, I really really have to take a pee. I contemplate the window, but don't think I can get it open wide enough to piss out. I work the screwdriver frantically, my leg shaking. I'm trying to stay calm. Impossible. I'm literally going to pee my pants if I don't get this door open in the next thirty seconds. I think about banging and screaming for Sarah, but I don't think she'd make it on time, even if she heard me and wanted to come. I continue to twist the screwdriver in vain while I look around the room.

I see the giant wooden bowl that Sarah's mom brought back from Africa sitting on the little table beside the couch. There's no time. I grab the bowl and toss its potpourri contents on the floor. I whip down my pants and underwear, kneel down, grab a fearful and half-shrivelled Marvin, and aim him into the bowl. It almost hurts coming out I have to go so bad. With mixed feelings of worry and relief, I watch the urine level rise in the bowl. With less than half an inch left in the bowl, I finish. I stand up and sigh in relief. Now that I'm not in a panicked state, I manage to pop the door open, no problem. I bend down, gingerly pick up the bowl, carry it very carefully to the bathroom, and dump it. I wash it out well with dish soap, put the bowl back, lie back down on the couch and fall asleep.

"Jesus Christ Colin, just because you're mad at me, doesn't mean you can just throw my stuff around. Why would you be so inconsiderate as to dump out my potpourri?"

I open my eyes. Sarah's dressed for work. My mouth is dry. My head hurts. I look at the dried-up flowers and leaves scattered on the floor and for a second I really don't remember. "I didn't throw... wait a minute. Sit down. I'm sorry. Please honey, I'm sorry. I have a story for you."

Reluctantly she sits down and listens while I explain what happened. She laughs quite hard at my tale of woe. I shower, and we go grab breakfast at Ada's Diner on Bank Street. I tell her over bacon and eggs the things I think she wants to hear. She seems to need my commitment verbalized. I tell her that I'm ready to be a father and have a family.

I don't lie about this. I want to be a father almost as much as I want to be a writer. Perhaps I want to fix my childhood by recreating it, reliving it, making it right. I don't share this part of my theory with Sarah. I promise to ease up on the drinking. Sarah worries because she loves me, though sometimes I think she worries about herself and projects it onto me. I've seen her crack back a couple bottles of wine on a Friday night.

I kiss her goodbye outside the restaurant and hop a bus to work.

Hungry Hole

Chapter 4

Ryan wasn't sure why he hadn't told Gillian about the hole. It was partly that he wanted to fix it himself, to prove he was capable of doing it, that he was a man. Mostly though, he didn't want Gillian to worry about it. She could stress over the littlest of things sometimes. Besides, he was worried enough for the two of them. Every day now, after Gillian left for work, he tested the levelness of the house with the marble. He went from room to room placing the marble in the middle of the floor to see if it would roll. Never anything. The house stood as erect and as level as ever. But the hole in the basement still seemed to be growing. It was now about four feet in diameter. Ryan had laid some two-by-fours across the hole so he could safely cross to the other side of the basement.

With trepidation, he slowly descended into the basement, flashlight in hand. The two-by-fours were still there, but now the bottom of the hole was no longer visible. He went to the edge and peered down. There was no end in sight. He clicked on the flashlight and shone the beam down. He still couldn't see the bottom. Ryan carefully lay down on his belly and peered over the edge with the flashlight to see if he could make out the bottom. The light of the flashlight ended in darkness. The wall of the hole was almost smooth, as if the whole thing had been drilled.

He reached into his pocket and found the marble he'd been using for his level tests. He dropped it down the hole. About three seconds later he heard a *ting*, followed by another one a second later, then it trickled off. *Ting, ting, ting.* "Bizarre," Ryan said aloud.

When he stood up, he heard the growl. At first he thought it was coming from the hole, but when he heard it the second time, he knew. He'd left the back door wide open when he put the garbage out, to get some fresh air into the house. He mustn't have shut the fence properly, for when Ryan looked up the stairs, his fears were realized. There was Spike, gums wet and quivering, saliva drooling from one corner of his powerful jaws.

"Nice Spike," said Ryan, holding his hand out in a gesture that he hoped the dog would sense was friendly. Spike barked and then barked a few more times before breaking back into a vicious growl. "Nice Spike," repeated Ryan as he put his foot on the bottom step. That's when he saw the muscles in the dog shift, saw it lean back, about to jump.

Ryan spun, squeezing by the handrail. The dog sailed into the air. Ryan ran toward the hole. The dog landed and spun when it hit the ground. The dog kicked its legs until it was up and moving again, moving in the direction of Ryan's back. Ryan misstepped. His foot landed in the middle of the two-by-fours, near the far edge of the hole. He lost his balance and he kicked back trying to keep his momentum moving forward. The result was that he managed to kick the two-by-fours into the hole as he fell with them. As he plummeted he felt the dog bite into his bum. Although the top half of Ryan hit the basement floor, his legs entered the hole. With the weight of the dog, which was now dangling off Ryan's right jean pocket by its teeth, Ryan was being pulled in. The paws of Spike clawed wildly away at Ryan's jeans, scratching him.

"Fuck!" screamed Ryan. "Get the fuck off!" He was being pulled into the hole when suddenly he heard the fabric rip. The pocket was coming off. He did his best to kick at the dog, trying to kick it in the balls. The fabric ripped again, this time completely. He felt the weight of the dog release. It was gone. He waited. Finally he heard a thud, followed by a whimper, then silence.

Ryan pulled himself out of the hole. He was shaking. Then came a strange sound from the hole, a kind of groan, but not that of a wounded animal. No, it almost sounded like a burp.

* * *

After Ryan changed his pants and cleaned the scratches on his legs, he went back down to the basement. He shone the light down the hole to see if there was any trace of the dog. Although he couldn't see the dog he saw something even more surprising: he saw the bottom, maybe a hundred feet down. The hole had receded. Had his eyes been playing tricks on him? Then a feeling of dread came over him. Maybe the hole was hungry.

The Catch-822 Photocopier

Today a branch-wide email was sent out about the photocopier. Things must have come to a head somewhere. Probably Barry started frothing at the mouth. He's a manager and his banality of leadership cascades down upon us every day like the drool off the chins of the institutionalized. Everyone suspects that he's behind the photocopier insanity. The email states that a virtual lock has been put on the copier and you now need a passcode to unlock it. Plus you need to fill out requisition form 822 stating the reason you need to make a photocopy.

I work for the government. I recognize it's insane, but sometimes I just can't believe it. I'm down to my last walkthrough 811 form. I need to make photocopies. I walk down the hall and head over to see Line, the secretary for the floor. Line lives in Gatineau, Quebec, just across the Ottawa River. She's always smacking her gum loudly when I come by. Half the time you can't find her because she's by the front door smoking with the other Francos who work on the floor. To be fair, there are two Anglos who also puff away, Brita being one of them and she smokes enough for four people.

Today Line's wearing white pumps with black nylons, a tight red leather skirt, and a white shirt with black polka dots. Her hair is eighties hair, combed up at the front and long and wavy in the back. You could fit your fist through her red hoop earrings. I can smell the pungent fumes of cigarettes off her clothes as I approach.

"Oui?" she barks out in her Gatineau French. She taps her watch and says, "It's noon thirty. It's time for my lunch, so you have to make it quick."

"I need the passcode for the photocopier."

"Didn't you read your email?"

"Yes, that's why I'm here."

"Where's your 822 form?"

"I don't have one."

"I thought you said you read your email?"

"Well I guess I need an 822 form then."

"Well I only have one 822 form, so you'll need to make a copy."

"Okay," I say, waiting for her to give me the form so I can photocopy it, so I can make a photocopy.

"You need to have an 822 to make a photocopy."

"What?"

"You need to have a ..."

"No, I heard you. So you're saying that to photocopy my 811, I need an 822 filled out, but to get an 822 I need to fill out an 822 so I can photocopy what I don't have."

"Yes," she says, staring at me like I'm an idiot, smacking her gum.

"Line, you can see how insane that is can't you? Why aren't these forms on the LAN so we can print them ourselves?"

"You have a problem with the system, take it up with Barry.

I'm just following orders."

"Orders? What is this, the military? Jesus, how am I to do any work?"

"Listen, Colin, it's time for my lunch. Here's what I suggest, you take ten dollars from petty cash and go to Office Land across the street in the mall and copy yourself some 811s and 822s."

"You have to be shitting me."

"You want the ten dollars? Cause I'm leaving."

"Fine."

She pulls a long thin beaded chain over her head and a silver key rises out from her deep and well-tanned cleavage. She unlocks her desk drawer, pulls out a small black box and fishes out a ten.

"Sign for it here in the book," she orders.

I sign.

"Make sure you bring back the receipt and the change," she says passing me the bill.

"Thanks. Can I also have your 822 to photocopy?"

"Borrow, not have."

"Right, just borrow. I promise I'll bring it right back."

"Make sure you do," she says, locking the drawer back up, the key dropping back into titty valley.

I walk back over to the mall. On the other side of Sunshine Valley Mall is Sunshine Valley Retirement Residence, hence the mall is always jammed up with old people. Here comes one of the regulars. She putters by in her pink bathrobe, riding a motorized scooter with an oxygen tank, plastic tubes up her nose. I have work I want to get done, so I'm annoyed that I have to dodge all these slowpokes. I know they can't help being old, it's more that the whole Catch-822 photocopier thing has got me pissed. As I grouch along, I see Phil sitting in one of the salon chairs at First Choice Haircutters. Zoe's washing his hair. I was just here with Phil only thirty minutes ago having lunch at The Shawarma Pit. He said he was going to stop in quickly and just say hi.

There seems to be only one girl working at the Copy and Print Centre of the store. Three people are in line ahead of me, including the young couple currently being served. The clerk is with them at a computer monitor looking at a picture of a longhaired orange and white tabby lounging on a sofa. They seem to be manipulating the picture. After five minutes of this, the clerk leaves and attends to a beeping machine. She feeds the machine a bundle of paper, then goes back to the young couple and presents them with different types of paper, which I presume the cat picture will be printed on. I'm about to lose my mind.

The old guy in front of me, who has a walker and one giant hearing aid, reeks of mothballs and pee. He twists himself around slightly, still leaning on his walker and asks me which bus I'm taking. "Where are you going? What bus?" he yells, little flecks of saliva sprinkling the air.

"I'm just getting some copies made," I tell him waving my 822 form in the air, hoping he understands.

"Kingston?" he yells back.

"No, *copies* made."

"Oh, Cobden. I have a niece who lives up in Cobden. I'm going to Montreal."

I realize that something is wrong. "This isn't the bus station," I yell so he can hopefully hear me.

The poor old guy looks confused. "Not the line for the bus?" he asks.

"No, you have to go out the mall and down the street."

"Oh," he laughs. "I thought this was the line for the bus."

I smile at him and nod my head and think, fuck, I never want to be that old.

He throws it into high gear and takes about two minutes to turn his walker around, then shuffles away. It'll be a miracle if he ever does make it to the bus station, let alone home.

After another painstaking ten minutes, the cat people finally finish up and get their print of Gingersnap. Why wouldn't they go to a photo shop? The lady who's now in front of me has a large and complicated order. She has a hefty briefcase and she pulls out fifteen small piles of paper. She needs things collated, bound, resized, stapled, etc. Her order takes twenty minutes. The line grows six people deep behind me while I wait. At one point I ask if there is anyone else around to help. The clerk tells me that Joey called in sick today. Super. Joey is probably jerking off at home with his X-Box.

I would have used one of the several manual printers, which are around me, but Line requires a goddamn receipt. Finally it's my turn.

"Hi, how can I help you?" asks the clerk in her friendliest voice. I must give her credit, she looks tired and overworked, but she's putting on a valiant show.

"Something simple for you, I just want this sheet photocopied."

"Just one copy?"

"No, make it ten. No wait, make it twenty."

"Twenty?"

When the clerk hands me back my sheets, I ask for a receipt. It's a quarter after one. Unbelievable. I pass by a pet store and see bunnies in the window. I think that Ryan, my character for *Hungry Hole*, will have to stop by and pick up a few – is that too dark? No, it's a horror story after all, just the same as my work.

At First Choice, Phil is now in Zoe's chair having his hair worked on.

I go to my desk, stash away my twenty copies of form 822 and then head to Line's desk. Crazy Larry is staring out the window as I walk by. "Okay, here's your 822, your change and the receipt," I say as I pass back everything. The stench of cigarettes wafts through the air indicating Line has just gone for yet another break.

"Merci," she says.

I go back to my desk and pull out the 822. The form is a crossword puzzle of boxes to fill in. Date. Time. Group ID#. Personal ID#. Name, first and last, my Project Leader's name, first and last, and my Manager's name, first and last. Number of copies requested. Reason for copy request. Approval of request signature box. Photocopy completion date and time. I don't know who's more nuts, the management or me, because I fill the whole thing out. Once I'm done, I bring it back to Line's desk. There's a little sign on her chair that says, *Back in five minutes*. I rub my temples and think about an imaginary hole in the basement of an imaginary house and what it should devour next.

I wait ten minutes before Line gets back. "Oui?" she asks.

"Here's my 822. Now, can I have the passcode please?"

"First you must have the form approved."

"By whom?"

"Barry, who else do you think?"

"Jesus. How long will that take?"

"He's in a meeting for the rest of the day, and tomorrow he's at a conference downtown, and then he's on vacation for a week."

"I should have just photocopied both forms while I was there."

"Mais oui," she says.

"Can I have five dollars from petty cash please?"

She pulls off the chain, gets the key, gets the box again, I sign the ledger and she hands me a five.

"Sure, just make sure you bring back the receipt and change."

By the time I'm back from Office Land the second time, it's 2:45. I'm so angry I could bust. I spend the rest of the afternoon writing an email to Bruce explaining what is wrong with the new photocopying procedure. Not that it will do any good, but I'm bitterly sarcastic and it makes me feel good.

I phone Sarah at work and she tells me that the fertility drugs are making her suffer something awful; she's dizzy and experiencing hot flashes. Moreover, the Metformin is giving her cramps. I tell her I love her and hope she feels better. I promise to make her a nice dinner. She tells me that she isn't hungry. I tell her I'll see her at home soon.

I think about pushing Barry and Bruce down my imaginary hole. I smile at this as I walk to catch my bus after work.

Days 11 to 22

Day 11

Sarah and I have been a couple for seven years now. The first year we dated long distance. She finished up her master's at Laval University and moved straight to Ottawa after. We've been living together for six years and have been married for five. Sarah and I have had lots of sex. Loads of sex. That first year we were together, every time she took the bus down to Ottawa, or I took it up to Quebec City, it was a sexual circus, and every night I was on the trapeze working without a net. If we weren't walking outside, or sitting in the pub, we were performing under the big top. We even made love in a park by the Museum of Nature, underneath the life-sized statues of the woolly mammoths. The thing about all this sex was it was fun, voluntary sex. We had no schedule. We were breathing each other in. When we touched it was the way a pianist would touch a Steinway; simple notes grew quickly into symphonies. Now we play "Chopsticks." Wagner has left the building.

So this is Day 11, actually it is the thirteenth day of the month, but the eleventh day on the drugs – the first day we're to have sex according to Dr. King's schedule. After we finish a home-cooked meal of spaghetti and meatballs, Sarah asks me if I want to do it. I'm a little irked by the way she asks. It's not playful or fun, but resonates with a harsh business tone. I recognize she hasn't been feeling well and our infertility issues always seem to be at the forefront of her mind. Still, if we're going to do it, then she could at least pretend she's interested, no? Somehow she seems to have sensed what I was thinking, or maybe she hadn't asked as coldly as I first thought, because she smiles a naughty smile and saunters over to me ever so slowly, undoing the buttons on her blouse. When she reaches me standing in the living room, she cups my crotch in her hand and bites me lightly on the neck. I feel Marvin fill with blood. I smell Sarah's hair and I become rock hard. She undoes my pants, pulls down my underwear, and pushes me backward onto the couch. She peels off her own panties, but leaves her skirt on, just hikes it a bit as she straddles me. Her shirt is open but her bra is still on. I play with her nipple through the black fabric. She throws her head back, mouth slack, moaning. Sadly after only a few minutes of this I can't take any more – it's been a few weeks since we made love. "Sorry honey, but I have to cum," I whisper to her.

Her eyes widen and she becomes focused, as if she's been faking it the whole time. "Quick, turn over, let me be on bottom," she says, getting off me. I do as she asks, then quickly get back in. The position change slows me down. "Aren't you going to cum?" she asks.

"Just give me a minute, will you?" She bites my ear. She knows I enjoy this. I cum.

"Wait," she says grabbing my ass, "don't pull out yet. Stay

inside a little longer. Make sure you get everything out."

So I do. "Are we good now?" I ask after a minute has elapsed.

"Yes, but pull out slowly, try not to suck any sperm back out."

"It's a penis, not a vacuum cleaner." She doesn't respond to this. As soon as I'm out, she kicks her legs high and braces her bum into the air with her hands on her hips, elbows and shoulders on the couch in a bicycle gym exercise form.

She turns her head to me, "Good work baby. I don't want to let any fall out. If you want, you can grab me by the legs and try to shake it down," she offers, bouncing her bum ever so slightly, trying to do just that, shake it down.

"I think you're probably good," I wheeze, pulling up my underwear and flopping back on one of the living room chairs.

"Is *Dateline* on tonight?" she asks me, legs still high in the air.

Day 12

After work we meet up at her favourite Italian restaurant in the Market, Mamma Grazzi's. After the first glass of wine, the stress of work leaves my body. "I fucking hate my job," I tell Sarah.

"I know baby. Why don't you look for something else?"

"I want to be a writer."

"I know honey. Why don't you try working for a newspaper or something?"

"Because I took computer science, not journalism."

"Why don't you write about computers for a computer magazine?"

"I'm sick to death of computers. I can't stand them. When you have to do something, it takes the joy right out of it."

At that moment the waiter comes by with our appetizer. When he leaves she asks me, "How's the new book coming along?"

"Fine, I guess."

"Why don't you write something different? A work of science fiction has never won the Giller."

"What are you talking about?"

"Maggie Woodland would never write a book like that."

"What are you talking about? She wrote *The Cranky Ox* and *The Latte Maid's Hand* – they're both science fiction."

"Yeah, but they definitely weren't her best. She'd never write something so, well, trashy."

I pour myself another big glass of wine. "Thanks for that."

"Oh, don't be mad, honey. I didn't mean trashy. I just don't enjoy science fiction."

"*1984, Brave New World*, those are great books, no?"

"They're okay."

"Okay, *1984* is just *okay*?"

"Honey," she tries to soothe. "Listen, if you don't want to look for another job, then you'll just have to keep writing and hoping for the best. I'm just not sure science fiction is the way to go."

"Fine."

"You're mad."

"No."

"Yes you are, I can tell."

"Whatever, let's just try to enjoy the meal."

We switch topics to going to see a film. So we hit the Bytowne Cinema after dinner and see some Italian comedy that neither Sarah nor I find particularly funny. We arrive home and another rejection letter is waiting in the mailbox. I'm pissed. I strip naked in the hall and tell Sarah to get undressed. I fuck her angrily and the sex is great. After I pull out, she moves into an upside-down bicycle. I find a bottle of wine and crack it open. I pour two glasses and sit naked in the dark in the living room. I wonder if I'm ever going to make it. In this moment, I foresee my life as a series of endless little tasks: tie your shoes, wait for the elevator, do your job, fuck your wife as you are told to. Sarah appears wearing just panties. Her beauty strikes me in such a way that it throws me off kilter, as if somebody called out my name for a prize I didn't even know I was nominated for. She grabs her glass off the coffee table as she sits beside me.

"It will happen."

"The book or the baby?"

"Both," she says.

Day 13

It's Saturday and I'm hungover, as I'm sure Sarah is, too. Whenever I'm hungover, all I want to do is screw and drink chocolate milkshakes. I smell Sarah's armpit and Marvin springs to life – I'm a rock.

"Come on baby, day thirteen," I tell her. She still has her eyes closed, but I can tell she's awake.

"Just get on me and do it, I'm not moving."

I pump away for some time, probably only about seven minutes before I finish. Sarah seems to be enjoying it near the end. When I pull out, she spins around and puts her legs up on the wall and says, "God, your breath is fucking awful."

"Thanks, sexy," I say smiling and happy.

"Make me a coffee, will you?"

I walk to the bathroom and piss away my morning erection.

As I pass by the bedroom doorway on my way to the kitchen, I ask, "French toast?'

"Sure," she says, her feet still planted on the wall.

Day 14

We go to our friends' place for brunch. They're big potheads; my characters Dean and Marsha in Hungry Hole are modelled after them. I suspect that they are stoned when we get there, but I don't think I could really tell either way. They are admitted chronics. They've just gotten used to being high all the time, and now they act just as normal as anyone else. Strange. We spend the rest of the afternoon touring the market, picking up a horn-of-plenty satchel of goods.

Arriving home, Sarah has a bath while I hit the kitchen to embark on food preparations. I'm slicing ginger for a chicken stir-fry when Sarah materializes in the kitchen doorway wearing unbelievably sexy red lingerie with black high heels.

"Come get some," she purrs.

I put down my knife and go get some.

Day 15

I arrive home late, almost 7:30, after a day of computer problems at the office. Sarah left work early today because she felt so lousy, and has been home alone for hours. The place looks like a dirty laundry bomb went off.

"How's it going baby?" I ask her.

"I feel just fucking awful on the drugs. I stood up at my desk and thought I was going to pass out. People say that all the time

74

but I'm not kidding you. My vision went blurry and I lost my balance. It was really scary."

"Anything I can do for you?"

"No. What do you want to do for dinner?"

"You didn't make anything?"

"Jesus, I've been lying down. I told you, I haven't been feeling well. Besides, I didn't know when you'd be home."

"Pizza?"

"Sure, I guess"

The pizza takes forever to show up. By the time I've cleaned up it's 9:30. We watch some bad reality TV until 11. When the show is over, Sarah says, "Don't forget, we have to have sex tonight."

I'm dead tired. I'd completely forgotten about our lovemaking schedule. "Right, let's get it on."

We disrobe, brush our teeth and hop into bed. Marvin is half-slouched against my balls. I tug at him a little to get him going. Sarah's hand slithers under the covers and pulls at Marvin a little too.

"What's wrong with Marvin?" she asks.

"Nothing, he's just tired."

"What, you don't find me attractive?"

"Jesus Sarah, no, I'm just tired. We've had sex every day for the last four days. It's just hard to turn on just like that."

"Nothing is hard here. We used to make love four times a day."

"That was seven years ago."

"So? Why aren't you getting hard?"

"Maybe because you're yelling at me?"

"Can you please hurry up and get hard, I have to work in the morning."

I play with my dick for a while. I try not to be angry. I think about the tight jeans of the attractive girl I saw on the bus. Marvin responds well to this image.

"Okay, I'm ready," I say.

"Okay, stick it in." I get it in, but I'm not all that hard. After a few strokes I firm up. I pump away forever.

"Are you almost done? I'm getting sore down there," Sarah says, or rather orders, the agitation in her voice evident.

I think about the ass on the bus. I think about Mrs. Dunbar, her tits. I cum.

I roll off.

"Goodnight," she says turning out the light, spinning around and putting her feet up against the wall.

Day 16

Sarah whispers a dirty story in my ear on the couch about her and another woman engaging in lesbian acts. Marvin loves it. We make love on the couch.

Day 17

I suggest a change of position, so we go at it doggy style. Sarah seems to love this. It works well for me too.

Day 18

Sarah had to leave work early again because she thought she was going to pass out. I suggest that we skip a day if she isn't feeling well, that the doctor said that we could. She tells me that Day 18 is critical for ovulation, that we have to do it. This have to business is killing me. The rebel in me doesn't want to have sex if he is ordered to.

"Look, I know you're finding this difficult too, so I went to the 7-Eleven and got you this," she says, passing me a copy of *Swank* magazine. A young blonde woman sucking on her own breast adorns the cover. Marvin sits up and pays close attention. It's not every day that your wife buys you porn and encourages you to read it. I believe she partly enjoys it, too, but I know she'd never admit to this. "Let's sit and read it together," she says, patting the couch beside her.

So I do.

"Wouldn't you love to fuck her?" she asks as she grabs my crotch.

Marvin's a little freaked out, but very excited. The next thing I know we're butt naked, going at it, two savages on the living room floor.

I roll off of Sarah, dripping in sweat. She scoots over to the wall and puts her legs up. "You did good, baby," she tells me.

"Thanks," I say, too tired to move.

Day 19

"Do you think this is going to work?" she asks.

"I hope so," I pant.

"You almost done?"

"Yep, just give me another second. Argh."

I roll off. Sarah moves into the vertical upside-down bicycle position.

Day 20

"Jesus, I thought you'd never finish."

"Me too," I groan.

"Just two more days, baby."

Day 21

We go to the sex shop and get inspired. She ties me up nice and tight. It's glorious.

Day 22

After work tonight, there's a farewell at the bar for Marc, a database guy who's heading off to PEI to work in another division. I tag along. Marc's a nice guy and I could use a beer. When I get home I'm a little drunk. Sarah's mood smells like it's in poor health.

"We have to have sex you know."

"Yeah, so?"

"When you drink you never cum, you take forever. God, you stink, how many pints did you have?"

"Four," I answer, telling her the truth.

"I want you to fuck me."

"Okay, let's go."

Marvin surprisingly springs into action. Things are going smoothly, but then after grinding away for ten minutes, I worry that I won't finish. I try to think sexy thoughts, Mrs. Dunbar's sweater, the nude witch on the broomstick... I involuntary flash to my grandmother's tits – yuck!

"Can you hurry up, please?"

"Relax, I'm trying."

"If you didn't drink so much, it wouldn't be a problem."

Marvin sags a little. I think about the glossy pages of *Swank*. I'm trying to focus on the girl-on-girl action when I become aware of Sarah's finger penetrating my asshole, stimulating the prostrate. Marvin can't take more than a few seconds of this before he erupts.

"Thank you," says Sarah, "try not to drink when we're supposed to be fucking." She spins around and puts her feet on the wall.

We go back to see Dr. King. It turns out that Sarah hadn't even ovulated. He ups her dose of Clomid and says that we will have to try again. "Remember, Days 11 to 22, lots and lots of sex."

The Paperless Office

From: Bruce Michaels
Date: 2006/07/08 PM 7:47:55 EDT
To: Colin MacDonald
Subject: Re: Photocopier Madness

Colin:
I understand your frustration with the photocopier; however change is never easy. Our world is changing at a rapid and sometimes frightening pace. The threat of global warming is upon us. That is why by 2012, we hope to reach the goal of "Paperless Office." Imagine Colin, a paperless office. No more filing cabinets, no more losing things, no more clutter. The trees would no longer be afraid. By 2012, the Ministry of Revenue Collection will be leading the world with our sustainable development. Our vision, our solution to the global-warming

problem: Paperless Office. This is why Barry and the rest of the management team have taken the first and crucial step in trying to reduce the amount of photocopying on the floor. In the near future there are plans to eliminate all but one printer, and eventually eliminate it completely.

Your suggestion for online forms to replace 811s, 822s, etc. is a good one. I will be bringing up this suggestion with Barry and the management team at our next weekly meeting. Your suggestion shows thinking "outside the box" and I have made note of this for your next performance review. Good job Colin! There will be more information coming out about "Paperless Office 2012." Remember, change is difficult, but it's easier if you think about it as *not staying the same*.

Thanks, Bruce

PS I left you a "Paperless Office 2012" pamphlet in your in-basket.

Part of me is laughing, and part of me is seething. Sure enough, I look over and there's the piece of paper Bruce left me about a paperless office. I grab it, without even so much as a glance, and throw it into my recycling bin. It appears that Carla is actually moving away from the paperless office. Usually she has nothing on her desk except for her hand sanitizer and occasionally an 810 or 811 and a pen. However, I've noticed in the past few weeks she no longer puts her pen directly on her desk; she puts it on a piece of clean white paper. I guess she just can't keep the desk clean enough.

Dan has probably killed more trees than Dutch elm disease.

His desk is covered in paper, sedimentary layers of government forms and tabloid magazines. Dan looks up from *Entertainment Weekly* and catches me staring at his desk. I'm doomed. "Hi Colin, working hard or hardly working?" he asks, laughing.

I'm not sure how to respond to something so inane and unfunny, so I ask him, just to be polite, "How's the tooth?" And as soon as the words leave my lips I know, but it's too late. I've dropped something fragile, my sanity. I watch it fall in slow motion, about to shatter into little pieces. Dan opens his mouth.

"Oh God Colin, it was horrible. The dentist had to fill two teeth. He said that he'd never seen an infection that bad in twenty years of practice. He told me I was very lucky I didn't have to lose the teeth. He worked on me for over an hour. And do you know what the kicker was, Colin?"

"No," I say, not wanting to answer.

"I was allergic to the antibiotics. I ended up in emergency covered in hives, having trouble breathing. They gave me different stuff, but the Tylenol-3 I was taking gave me terrible constipation and it ripped my hemorrhoids to shreds."

I wave my hands in front of my body and say, "No, no, no, too much information."

Although Dan laughs at my reaction, it seems to spur him on. "I tell you Colin, I had to see the doctor about my hemorrhoids after because the pain was so great. I had to get a cream with a steroid in it to settle things down. Oh God, the burning and itching was intense I tell you."

"Jesus Dan," I say, but he keeps going, telling me next about his bad back, his slipped disc. For the next half hour he talks about how he's going to acupuncture for his crooked foot, and the physiotherapy he had to go through last fall for his rotator cuff.

"I'm a mess, Colin."

"Sounds like it. Look I gotta hop," I tell him, leaving our quad, not sure of my destination, only of my escape.

I walk out and see a plumber putting a sign on the men's washroom door, *Out of Order*. "Busted pipe, you'll have to use the handicapped washroom or go to a different floor," he tells me.

"Actually, I'm just walking by." I do a loop around the floor, walking aimlessly. I think about Sarah. The fertility treatment has been extremely difficult for her. I hope she ovulated after this second round of treatment. I can't go through a third round of 11 to 22. I walk over to the Sunshine Valley Mall to grab a coffee and give her a call to see how she's doing. I realize I've left my cellphone on my desk, but there is no way I'm going back for it. Of course when I get to the mall, both pay phones are being used. I go get my coffee first. When I get back, the same people are still on the pay phones. The young girl in the Hannah Montana T-shirt seems to be chatting with a girlfriend. Shouldn't she have a cellphone? I'm one to talk. The business man seems to be dictating instructions to his secretary. They're both babbling strong.

Finally after another five minutes, the business guy gets off. Both the phone handle and earpiece are warm. I think of Carla and the prime breeding ground for bacterial growth that I'm holding. I fish for quarters and dial.

"Sarah MacDonald."

"Hi, it's me."

"Why aren't you calling from your desk or the cell?" she asks.

"Walked to the mall, forgot the cell on my desk. I needed a break. The place is driving me nutso. How ya doing, baby?"

"Remember how I was having that weird feeling on Day 25?"

"Yeah."

"Well I think it could be implantation in the uterus."

"Really?"

"Do me a favour, go to the pharmacy and pick me up a pregnancy test."

"Really?" I say excited.

"I'm not sure; don't get your hopes up."

As I walk to the pharmacy, my mind is popping and flashing, like I'm flipping channels on the TV. The noise of the shoppers and the shopping-mall lighting contribute to my disorganized thoughts. I could be a dad. I might have fathered a child. As I pass through the turnstile I read a headline from the newspaper stand: "Man Dies in Head-on Collision." We'll need to get an infant car seat. How much do they cost?

I find the aisle with the pregnancy tests and decide to go with the generic pharmacy brand, a two-for-one pack. If it's negative, I figure we can use the second test next month if we need to. If she is pregnant, I know that she'll want another test to double check.

As I pay for the kit, I make sure to smile that extra little bit, so the clerk knows that I'm hoping for a positive result, rather than the poor bastard who's hoping for a negative one so he doesn't have to head off to the Morgentaler clinic. The clerk puts the kit into the bag after scanning it. She doesn't even look at it. I stop smiling so hard.

I walk back to my building. As I approach the main door, I see Line arguing with a man transporting twenty large boxes on a flatbed dolly.

"Listen lady, I just drop the stuff off. This is what the order says. I'm just doing my job."

"What's up?" I ask Line.

"I ordered one box of each colour of file folder, but it says I ordered one flat of each colour. He showed me the form, and it's true. I checked the wrong box. But why would anyone want a flat of file folders. You figure common sense, no?"

"This is the government, Line."

"True," she says taking a long haul off her menthol smoke.

"How many colours are there?"

"Ten," she laughs.

I catch the guy with the flatbed and ride up with him in the elevator. "That's a lot of file folders."

"You're telling me, Mack," says the guy.

I follow the guy out of curiosity, just to see it with my own eyes. We pass by Crazy Larry who is standing up as per usual, but instead of looking out the window he's looking at us coming down the hallway.

"Hi buddy," says the delivery guy to Crazy Larry.

"Hi," Crazy Larry says, really slowly like he is stoned.

"What's his problem?" the delivery guy whispers to me after we pass.

"He's crazy."

"Yeah, no shit."

When we arrive at the business centre, I can barely believe my eyes. The length of one wall, about sixteen feet, is already covered in boxes, four boxes high, two rows deep. The delivery guy unloads, making a third row. "Wow," I say.

"Yeah," the guy says. "Got three more flats still in the truck."

I look at all the boxes of file folders in disbelief.

I go back to my desk and I hear Dan telling the exact same story he told me about his tooth and the rest of his medical adventures to somebody three cubicles down. I glance over and notice the memo on Paperless Office 2012 in my recycle bin. I pick it out, march back to the coffee room and tape it to the wall above the hundreds of boxes of file folders.

Hungry Hole

Chapter 6

For a week now, Ryan had been going from pet store to pet store buying rabbits. One at a time at first, then later two at a time as he grew tired of making multiple trips. The hole seemed to enjoy the rabbits. It would retreat a bit, fill up. Two rabbits would make it shrink a lot. But after a few days, it didn't seem to make any difference. It was hungry; it wanted more.

Ryan had just tossed another rabbit in the hole when he heard the doorbell ring. He went upstairs and opened the door. It was Bill from next door. "I know you have Spike," he said.

"What?" replied Ryan, thinking to himself that there was no way Bill could know.

"I can hear him barking. I listened at your basement window and I heard him barking."

"No you didn't," said Ryan, but just as he said that he heard the unmistakable growl of Spike coming from the open basement door.

"I'm getting my dog," said Bill, pushing Ryan out of the way.

The barking grew louder as Ryan followed Bill toward the basement door and down the stairs. "You son of a bitch, I'm going to call the cops on you," yelled Bill as he ran.

Ryan didn't say anything. He just followed, curious to see if there was an actual dog there, or whether the hole was playing a game, luring Bill in. When Ryan got to the bottom, Bill was standing by the edge yelling, "Spike, I'm here boy." He spun around to Ryan. "You son of a bitch, you get my dog out of that hole!" screamed Bill, pointing down. Ryan was about to explain that there was no dog, at least he didn't think there was, when the earth under Bill's feet gave away.

"Aaahhhh!" Bill yelled as he dropped into the hole, but he managed to catch the edge with one hand. Flailing away, he grabbed the ledge with the other hand. Bill was now dangling by his fingertips. For a second, Ryan stood frozen. He thought about stepping on Bill's fingers, thought about feeding him to the hole. But quickly his mind cleared. He grabbed Bill's arm and said, "Don't worry, I have you."

"You son of a bitch, when I get out of here you're a dead man!"

"Relax, give me your arm. Grab on so I can pull you out."

When Bill let go of the edge and grabbed Ryan's hand, that's when they both heard it. It made the sound that water makes coming down a garden hose when you turn on the tap, except louder. It shot up out of the darkness, a purplish red tongue-like tentacle, wrapping itself around Bill's left leg.

"Aaahhhh!" Bill screamed again. "What the fuck is it? Get it off!"

I don't know, just hold on," Ryan said. Ryan saw the tentacle twist and contract. Ryan didn't have a chance to save him. Bill was ripped away in a flash.

Ryan heard one last scream before a small fountain of blood shot up out of the darkness dowsing him in a fine spray. He sat there frozen. There were no longer any dog sounds coming from the hole, but instead a noise that sounded vaguely like chewing. He slowly backed away on his hands and knees until he reached the foot of the stairs. Shaking, he stood up and walked upstairs to clean off the blood.

Two months later…

Estimates

I wake up to the now familiar sound of Sarah retching in the toilet. I stop in the doorway of the washroom on my way to the kitchen. She's on her knees, holding her hair up so it doesn't dangle into the toilet. Her back ripples and her neck extends forward. Her mouth opens, but nothing comes out but a sick groan. She reminds me of a cat trying to cough up a hairball.

"You okay?"

She nods.

"Do you want me to make you a coffee?"

She shakes her head no.

"Tea and melba toast?"

She nods again.

"I'm on it," I tell her as I move to the kitchen. I make myself a coffee and read the paper. I hear the bath start up. Sarah has actually lost weight during the first two months of pregnancy. The vomiting began two weeks after she peed on the stick. When Sarah gets out of the tub, I hop in and shower. Once I'm dressed for work, I go out to the living room. Sarah is sitting on the couch looking extremely pale, her untouched green tea and melba toast sitting on the coffee table in front of her. "You okay?"

"I think I might be sick again," she says, standing up and heading for the washroom.

I hear more retching sounds.

"I'm going to go, okay honey, unless you need me?" I yell down the hallway.

"Just go, I'll be fine in a few minutes," she mutters weakly.

On the bus I snag a window seat. A man with a huge beer gut sits down beside me. I'm pretty sure he hasn't seen his dick in years. He has some wicked coffee breath and reeks of cigarettes. Not surprisingly, Sarah hates taking the bus these days. One whiff of this guy and he would have a new appreciation for morning sickness. As the bus sways along its route, its lumbering metal structure rocks me into a state of sleepy complacency. The engine purrs, "Shhh Colin, go to sleep." I close my eyes. Blobs of light dance on the dark of my inner eyelids. I think about *Invasion of the Body Snatchers* and bolt upright in my seat, eyes wide. My mind floats to the laundry and dishes in the sink that need washing. I drift to other things I need to get done, the book I'm writing. Is it scary enough? Should it have a dark ending or should it have a little redemption?

I glance around me. There's a man seated across the aisle with hunched posture, a wilted flower. He gives the impression that the attrition of a bureaucratic routine has left him empty. A Tupperware container is perched atop his briefcase. I imagine him on this bus for the next twenty years, microwaved lunches, the same job. I imagine him slipping a noose around his neck and jumping off his Arborite kitchen counter, his flailing arms knocking over his Tupperware leftovers, little macaronis spilling out onto the floor. I see myself as him. I see myself trapped in my day job, trapped in the relentless predictability of it all. Maybe the ending of my new book should be dark?

But then the bus saunters to a stop and picks up a pregnant woman. Another woman moves to give her a seat. I stare at her swollen belly. I think about how much I love Sarah, ride this bus for her, eat the mircowaved banality for her – for her and my unborn child. But is love enough to keep riding this bus for the next twenty years? Maybe. Maybe not. I need to write my way out of it. Not that I want to, but I don't see another way. Maybe my book could use a little redemption? Maybe I could use some myself?

When I finally get into work and into my quad, Brita's there wearing black military boots, green army pants and a black T-shirt with a picture of Kurt Cobain on the front. She has shaven her head completely bald, reminding me of Sigourney Weaver in *Alien 3*. She's placing her personal possessions, including a Karl Marx action figure, computer manuals, CDs and various leftist magazines into a cardboard box.

"Where are you going? Are you switching groups?" I ask.

"Fuck that MacDonald, I quit this shithole. Let the capitalists find another lackey henchwoman to replace me. I'm off to the rainforest to stop deforestation. I'm going to blow up a few bulldozers. I'm going to straighten shit out."

"Wow, sounds like you're doing your part for Paperless Office 2012."

"Don't get smart with me, MacDonald," she threatens, swinging around with her box of junk.

"Well, good luck," I say extending my hand.

She looks at my hand and debates it. She decides to balance the box on one knee and quickly shakes. "You are one of the few people in here who isn't a complete asshole."

"Thanks," I reply, because I'm not sure what else to say.

"If I were you, MacDonald, I'd get out before this place takes your soul," she whispers leaning in toward me, so close I worry she might kiss me. Suddenly she spins around and yells at Carla, "Here is something for you, cunt!" spitting a glob of saliva onto Carla's flat-screen monitor, and then storming off. Carla sits frozen, looking completely horrified, staring at the sliding spittle as if it were a scorpion crawling down her screen. I almost laugh, but it seems like an unnecessarily cruel action, especially since Carla had done nothing to provoke her. I know the smell of cleaning products had always been a sore point with Brita, but considering Carla's condition, so to speak, I was surprised. Still, I think every person who has come into this quad has wanted to spit on Carla's desk, just to see what she would do. I'm looking at the answer and it's not pretty.

"Why did she do that?" she squeaked.

"I don't know, Carla. She's just mad at everyone and everything I guess." For the next hour, Carla goes into a hyper-animated cleaning frenzy, spraying and wiping everything down, over and over. The monitor gets at least a half an hour dedicated to itself alone.

Bruce waltzes in and grabs the guest chair that the four of us, now three of us, share in the quad. "Hey, smells clean in here. I guess you heard about Brita, eh?"

"She told me she quit."

"Wow, did she ever," says Bruce, but he fails to elaborate on what he means. After the spitting action, I imagine that Bruce got something equally as good. Bruce suddenly rubs his hands feverishly together as if he was trying to spark a fire, and then, in what I think he thinks is dramatic, slaps his knees. "Well, Colin, I'm afraid you'll have to be the one to pull up the slack around here until we find a replacement for Brita."

"Sure thing," I say, completely unfazed by what he's just said.

"Really?"

"Yeah, no problem."

Bruce seems flustered by my response, and I imagine he was waiting for me to take exception to what he's said so he'd have the opportunity to practise his manager skill set. I suspect he's got a performance review looming and he is looking for some examples of leadership to write down.

"Well you're going to have to refill out your estimates form, now that you're taking over for Brita ... temporarily that is."

Although I pretty much despise everything about my job, the one thing I hate above all others is doing estimates. I'm supposed to guess how much time it will take me to complete each piece of code that I'll be working on over the next six months. Now I'm going to have to figure out how much time doing two jobs will take. Dutiful, I do it just the same, for I am a good civil servant.

I work on my new estimates, form 220, for over two hours, trying to piece together everything Brita had been working on and would have been working on in the future. When I'm done, I bring the form over to Bruce. He's on the phone, so I drop it into his in-basket. Forty minutes later Bruce returns with the estimates form.

"You're a little high in a couple of places, Colin, and a little low in others. Look at it again, see if you can identify the problem areas, and fix them up."

"Sure thing," I say, seething on the inside. I go over the whole thing again and make what I think are the appropriate adjustments. When Phil and I get back from lunch I notice that the form is back in my in-basket with several yellow stickies on it identifying the areas where the numbers are too high or too low. My jaw tightens and I grind my teeth. I randomly beef up or down the numbers identified as being incorrect guesses and march it back to Bruce's desk. He's on the phone again, so I toss it into his in-basket.

Not ten minutes later, he's back in my quad. "Still not right Colin, a couple of these are still a little low."

"Well, why don't you just put the number that you want in the box?"

"Well Colin, then I would be doing your job, wouldn't I?"

I want to pop him in the mouth. "Bruce, I don't know what number should go in the box. It's an estimate. So just put in whatever number you want. I don't mind being wrong. I'm just tired of guessing."

"Colin, it's great practice for you. It'll help you. Just do your best, that's all I'm asking," he urges, putting the sheet back in my in-basket.

Insanity. But I smell something fishy here, aside from Bruce's power games. Bruce isn't that smart. I erase the numbers in question and put in new random numbers. I walk the 220 form over to Bruce's cubicle again. "That was quick Colin. Do you think you got it right this time?"

"You tell me."

"Well let me look it over and I'll bring it back if it needs fixing."

"Well just look at it now."

"Listen Colin, I have to finish this email, but I'll do it right after that."

I'm contents-under-pressure, a steaming kettle, Fahrenheit four-fifty-fuck-you. There's a worm in the apple and it's time to go fishing. "Fine," I say and leave, but I don't go far. I slip into Peter Cann's cubicle, right next door to Bruce's. I place my index finger to my lips and make a silent *shhh* to Peter. He's a good sport and doesn't say anything, just curiously watches. I stand on his guest chair and peer over the wall at Bruce. He's not writing his email. He's looking at my 220 form. He opens one of his desk drawers and pulls out two other 220 forms. I recognize one as my original from March 2006, and the other one I surmise to be Brita's. He's added them together to make sure they match my new estimates.

"Bruce!" I yelp over the wall. He jumps as if his spine were about to pop out of his back. I step down off the chair, thank Peter and spin around the light grey cubicle dividing wall and back into Bruce's cube. "Give me that," I demand snatching my 220 form from his hand. I quickly do the addition of all four boxes in question right there. It takes me about forty-five seconds and Bruce doesn't say a peep. When I'm done, I hand Bruce the form and say, "Estimates are now complete." I walk back to my cube with joy in my heart.

When I get to the office the next day there is a calendar invite from Barry, the manager, Mr. Paperless Office. He has requested a meeting with me at 10 a.m. in his office, the subject line: The Committee. I click the button to accept and don't think any more about it.

At 9:55 I get a pop-up reminder about the meeting. I hit the washroom, and then walk to Barry's office. When I get there, he waves me in and asks me to shut the door. Barry's a fat little man, habitually adorned in a light grey suit (almost the same colour as our cubicle walls – sort of office camouflage, so he can sneak up on people) and some sort of novelty tie. I think he's about fifty-five, but he seems to have no imminent retirement plans. It's not because he *has* to work; no, I think Barry has lots of money. He won't retire because he loves his job. He loves his job because he thinks he's making a difference. He thinks his job is important. Today his tie has a profile picture of

Homer Simpson drinking a Duff beer. I suspect that this tie, at least in Barry's mind, is a kind of jovial catalyst, a springboard to you-can-talk-to-me-for-I'm-a-man-of-the-people, just a small piece of his open-door managerial style that he professes as part of his office philosophy. "I hear that there was a bit of an incident yesterday with the work estimates."

"Yeah, Bruce is driving me crazy with those. I don't know what to tell you. The whole thing boggles the mind."

"Listen," says Barry, rolling his chair closer to mine, putting one hand gently on my knee. "Bruce was quite scared by what happened yesterday. He said, and this is a quote, he said he 'felt physically threatened' yesterday when you grabbed the piece of paper from his hand."

I'm stunned. "You have to be kidding me?" I ask.

"This is a serious matter Colin. Now I know that Bruce can be difficult sometimes, but he means well. I told him I'd have a talk with you. Now I think it would be best if you two were to communicate by email for a while, just to cool things down. I don't want you to have a black mark on your so-far spotless record, Colin. You're a good employee, Colin; just don't let your temper get to you."

I can't believe what I am hearing.

"Listen, Colin, let's forget the whole thing shall we? How about we get you involved in a special project?"

It occurs to me that if Barry were to gain fifty more pounds, put on a black suit, and stuff cotton balls into his mouth he might pass for a silly version of the Godfather.

"What favour?"

"I want you to join the Refrigerator Committee."

I think I should take this shit up with the union, but I really don't want the hassle. I don't want to be labelled as difficult. With no prospect of a million-dollar book deal on the horizon,

I need to keep my job, despite the fact that I loathe it with all of my being. With a child on the way, I don't want any "blemishes" on my record. "The Refrigerator Committee?"

"We need a new fridge in the coffee room. The Coffee Club Committee is swamped right now, so they set up another committee to purchase a new fridge. You'd help to raise money, you know, bake sales, raffle tickets, things of this sort. They're short one member, and so I volunteered one more person from my section – that would be you. Are you up for it?"

"Fine."

"Great, the first meeting is next week. Good luck with it. And remember, no more fighting with Bruce," he adds with a wink and a smile.

The Refrigerator Committee. Son of a bitch.

Two months later…

A Very Hungry Hole

We went for the third ultrasound today. It's a girl! We debated about finding out the gender, but Sarah just couldn't wait. She wants to get the room ready and wants the right colour on the wall. So I'm losing my study to Sam. Samantha, but I prefer Sam, or Sammy. Some might think of it as more of a boy's name, but I think Sammy is cute. So does Sarah. Seeing the head and hands today, not just the blip of a heartbeat, really brought it home that I'm going to be responsible for the development of a human life. The weight of it is pulling at me, a bungee umbilical cord tugging me off the edge of an egotistical tower and into the abyss of accountability. Thank heavens I have Sarah; at least I can only fracture half the child. I've talked about this with Sarah at length and she thinks I'm a good candidate for Xanax. She's told me repeatedly that I'm going to be a great dad, that she's seen me with her sister's children and I'm wonderful. I remain pessimistically nervous.

House of Won Ton brings us half their menu. When we went to the doctor's office, Sarah was actually down five pounds from her normal weight before pregnancy. Tonight something clicked inside her body and she's making up for lost time. Three spring rolls, a won ton soup, half an order of beef and black bean sauce, almost a whole order of lemon chicken and enough rice to stuff a suitcase. She drains back a tall glass of coke and lets out a humongous he-man belch. "Excuse me," she says.

"Wow, feel good?"

"Great. I've never felt better."

Two hours after the gorging, we're on the couch watching TV when a commercial for potato chips appears. Sarah leans forward, fixated, and asks, "Are you hungry?"

"No, you?"

"Starving. You know what I could really go for right now? Those nachos with the fake orange cheese."

"Like at the movies?"

"Yeah."

"Well I'm not going to the movie theatre just to get you chips."

"7-Eleven has them. Please?"

I walk the four blocks down to the 7-Eleven in the rain. It's blowing and friggin' cold as a witch's tit, which seems appropriate because most houses still have their Halloween decorations up. I should've brought my umbrella.

The door BINGs as I enter and my body welcomes the neon warmth of the store. I find the nacho-cheese machine on the back wall. Beside it, on a wire stand, sit black plastic containers with clear see-through tops which reveal their round salted nacho-chip contents. I look at the little white expiry stickers and they all say best before yesterday. I look over at the cash and there's only one person on with a line of five people deep and there seems to be nobody else in the store to help me with getting some fresh chips. I figure they're only chips, that one day can't make much difference. So I grab the container with the most chips and pop the lid off. There's a little pocket in the corner of the tray in which to pump your cheese. I place it under the nozzle and push the round spring-loaded button. Cheese trickles out, slow and thin. Then it stops altogether. I hit it a few more times only to get a few more drops. The pocket of the tray is only a third full, if that.

I look around for help, but there isn't any except the girl working the cash. I suspect this fluorescent orange cheese contains no dairy, but instead is made up of some edible oil product. I'm embarrassed to be buying it, let alone having to go up to the cash and ask for help with the busted machine. The line is down to three people and I wait patiently, not wanting to barge in and draw attention to myself. While I wait, three people come into the store. BING. BING. BING. I think, please don't line up behind me. But sure enough, Mr. Heavy Metal gets in line behind me right away. I assume he just wants cigarettes. For a fraction of a second I consider letting him go ahead of me, but then I realize I'll never get service if I do. Finally I stand before the young girl who has purple dreadlocks fastened atop her head with a black piece of ribbon adorned with white skulls. She has multiple piercings in her face: eyebrow, lip, nose, twenty in the ears. Her nametag reads "Angie." I meekly present my nacho tray to her and inform her that the machine is broken or out of cheese.

"Probably out of cheese. Just a second, I'll get Derek. I think he should be finished his break by now," she says as she leaves her post and presumably goes to find Derek, her purple pineapple hairdo bobbing as she goes. Two more people join the line. People are giving me the eye. They likely think I'm stoned and have the munchies – who else would eat this stuff?

Undernourished pregnant women, that's who.

Angie finally returns and says, "Just wait by the machine. Derek will be out in a minute with the cheese."

"Thanks," I say, sheepishly moving out of the line which has grown by another two people.

The brown storage room door suddenly swings open and a long lanky kid emerges, his arms wrapped around a large bag of orange cheese goo like a small child carrying a squirming puppy dog. "Hi," is all he says as he pops open the machine, removes the old bag and throws in the new one.

"Thanks," I say.

"Give it five minutes to heat up."

"Thanks," I say again.

"Right," he says, then heads up to the cash to help Angie.

I stroll over to the small rack of paperbacks, which is a mishmash of courtroom thrillers, Harry Potter books and Harlequin romances. I grab *Bedded by the Prince Warrior* and thumb through it: *As I tugged violently on his leather buttons, exposing his scarred, hardened, warrior chest, he released his belt and his sword fell to the ground, only to expose his other rod of steel. I could feel the battle about to rage...*

Good grief. Is this where the money is? Maybe I should write a romance book for the cash? I put back the book and return to the cheese machine, grab my chips, and hit the button again. A thick stream of hot cheese flows out. I fill the pocket and I also coat the chips as Sarah instructed before I left. "Make sure to get lots and lots of cheese." I release my thumb but the button doesn't seem to retract. The cheese continues to pour out. I try to grab the button and pull it back. I do. The button comes off in my hand; the cheese is continuing to pour out. Son of a bitch. I pull the chip tray away, and the catch basin of the machine fills quickly. I grab a coffee cup from the neighbouring counter and place it under the nozzle.

"Derek!" I yell. Everybody in line turns and stares over at me.

"Button broke, we have a problem here," I tell him. Derek sees the cheese pouring out and bolts back over to me. He pops the lid of the machine and knocks the coffee cup with fake cheese goo to the ground. "Sorry, I don't know what happened. The button was stuck and I tried to unstick it, and the darn thing just came off in my hand."

Derek doesn't say anything, he just continues to fiddle with the guts of the machine. With the lid open, there is no way I can put another cup under the nozzle. The cheese is continuing to flow down the counter and is pooling into a Cheez Whiz lake on the floor. There's nothing I can do except stand there and provide moral support to Derek while the people in line continue to stare. I turn red with embarrassment. Should I just keep standing here? I decide that there's no point and join the back of the line. When it's my turn to pay, Angie gives me an angry look. I pay. I dash quickly back out into the rain, the hot cheese fogging up the clear plastic top as I go.

Sarah pops a chip dripping with cheesy slime into her mouth and coos with excitement. "Thanks baby," she says, "you're the best. Do you want one?"

"No thanks."

"Oh God they're good," she tells me, shovelling another chip into her mouth.

"I'm glad they're tasty."

"Did you remember the chocolate bar?"

"Ah shit, sorry. There was a problem with the cheese pump thingy and I forgot."

"Oh that's okay, don't worry about it," she says, but I can tell she's a little disappointed. Normally I wouldn't have gone back out, not after all that, not when it's raining and cold out, but I've just spent four months watching the woman I love yack her guts out. Now she's eating. Maybe not the healthiest food on the planet, but at least it's something. Who am I to deny the mother of my child a simple candy bar? Little Sammy needs to eat. "I'll go back."

"Don't be silly, it's fine, really," she says.

"I'm going to get you that chocolate bar. I'll be back in a second," I say putting my coat on, grabbing my umbrella, heading out the door.

By the time I reach the 7-Eleven, the wind has made a pretzel out of my cheap umbrella. Two of the rods have snapped and I'm not much drier than I would have been without it. A homeless man is standing beside the garbage can where I stuff the umbrella.

"Spare some change?" asks the man.

I fish into my pocket and pull out a loonie.

"Thanks," he says as BING, I go through the door.

As I grab a Snickers bar off the rack, I look up and see a note taped to the cheese machine: *Out of Order.* Derek has the mop bucket out. I avoid his gaze and get into line. When it's my turn, Angie gives me another nasty glare.

"That everything?" she asks.

"Yes, just the candy bar."

"That will be a dollar fifteen."

I reach into my pocket and quickly come to the horrible conclusion that I only have thirty-five cents, after having given my last dollar away to the homeless man on my way in.

"Can I Interac that?"

"There's a five-dollar minimum," she spits.

"Can I do cash-back?"

"No, there's a cash machine over there if you need money."

"Fine," I say, leaving the bar on the counter. "I'll be right back." I return outside and see that the homeless man is still there, trying to light a bent cigarette butt. "Hi," I say.

"Hi," he says. "Spare any change?"

"Actually, I just gave you a dollar when I went in, just a minute ago."

He squints at me. "I don't know you," he says.

"I just gave you a dollar. I'm the guy who put the umbrella in the garbage."

"Yeah, what do you want?"

"I was wondering if I could have my dollar back. I'll give you the rest of my money, which is twenty cents. I know it's not much, but I really need my dollar back."

The man grumbles and fishes out a loonie. "Here ya go, cheapskate," he says, passing me back the coin.

"Thanks, sorry about that."

The line moves slowly. When I finally get to Angie, she says robotically, "Will that be everything?"

"Yes."

"A dollar fifteen. Bag?"

"No thanks."

By the time I get home, I'm frozen to the bone. "Here you go baby," I say, noting that Sarah has managed to polish off the nachos.

"You're so sweet," she says, giving me a kiss.

"I'm going to take a hot shower and do some writing, okay?"

"Bye," she says, unwrapping the bar.

Hungry Hole

Chapter 8

When the doorbell rang, Ryan was a little nervous. There before him stood the six-foot-two construction worker who had given Ryan his card. He was wearing the exact same thing as before: white construction hat, jeans, plaid shirt and beige steel-toed boots. "Hi Doug," said Ryan. "Please come in."

"It's Ryan, right?" asked Doug, extending his hand. Ryan grabbed Doug's hand, felt the calluses of years of hard manual labour.

"Ryan, that's right. Come on in. Boy oh boy, do I have something to show you." Ryan led the way.

"House looks pretty level on the outside. Seems good here in the hall."

"That's the strange part about it," said Ryan, turning on the light at the top of the basement stairs. "It is level. I check it every day. But this hole just keeps getting bigger." The sound of wind echoing down a tunnel grew louder as they reached the bottom.

"Jesus, what's that sound?" asked Doug.

"That's the hole. Crazy, isn't it?"

"Holy macaroni, can I borrow your light?" asked Doug.

Ryan stepped to the side, handing Doug the flashlight. He moved to the edge and peered down.

"I don't think I've ever seen anything quite like..."

Ryan didn't hesitate. He threw a bodycheck with his shoulder, hitting Doug in the lower back. Doug screamed as he fell in. There was a thud, followed by the sounds of chewing. The crunching sounds of chips being eaten.

"What are you doing baby?" Sarah asks, kissing my neck softly.
 "Writing."
 "You've been a very nice boy today. Why don't you come to bed and get a treat?"
 "Okay, just give me a minute to finish off my thoughts here."
 "Hurry, because this is a limited-time offer. I'm feeling sleepy."
 I type quickly.

All of a sudden a spray of blood shoots from the hole, spitting along with it Doug's bloodied pair of boots, hat, and Ryan's flashlight. The flashlight lands at Ryan's feet with a clunk, illuminating his stocking toes.
 Ryan knew he was going to need more food soon. A lot more.

Two months later...

Sitting Duck Press
222 Lark Avenue
Ottawa, ON
K1H 7C7

January 15, 2007

Dear Mr. MacDonald:

We regret to inform you that our publishing calendar is full for
the next three years.

Thank you for your interest in our press.

Best of luck with your writing.

Regards,

Simon Gibson
Editor

The Refrigerator Committee

I spent the holidays getting Sammy's room ready. It's goodbye to my writing study. I moved a third of my books into the bedroom and a third into the living room, and hauled two boxes of books to the second-hand bookstore. I put my writing desk into our storage unit in the basement and bought a tiny, crappy, thirty-dollar computer desk from Ikea for the living room. The couch was put out on the street corner. The room got repainted light pink with white trim. A new blind and curtains for the window went up. I assembled the crib my mother bought us. Then I assembled the change table that Sarah's mother bought us. Sarah's mother and my mother are in a competition to see who can give the baby more stuff. Christmas was an onslaught of everything baby. We now have dozens of sleepers and bibs adorned with cutesy expressions: "If you think I'm adorable, you should see my Grandma," "Please pass the bottle" and "Spit Happens." Sarah hasn't even had her baby shower yet.

We had my father and his third wife over for New Year's Eve dinner. He brought a giant stuffed bear with a red ribbon, which now sits in the corner of Sammy's room. He got drunk, insulted Sarah, then his new wife, and then told me that he always thought I would never amount to much. It was a good time. Work, on the other hand, was particularly miserable. Since I've joined the six-person Refrigerator Committee, life has been shit. I've been organizing bake sales, trying to "cash in on the Christmas market" as one of the geniuses of the committee put it. Today I'm off to our semi-monthly meeting on how we can turn fundraising around in the post-holiday season.

I walk into the boardroom. I'm the last to arrive.

"Hi Colin, I saved you a seat," offers Steve, patting the seat next to him even though there are only six of us in a ten-chair boardroom. Steve is flamboyantly gay.

"Thanks," I say, sitting down next to him.

"Okay, shall we begin?" asks Debra. Debra is an uptight bean-counter and the head of the committee. "Jill, can you give us an update on where we're at?" asks Debra.

"Wait, who's taking minutes?" pipes in Laura. Laura always takes the minutes. She actually types them up after each meeting and sends them to all the committee members and carbon copies the managers. I always delete them without reading.

We all just look at each other and nobody says anything. "Okay, I guess I'll do it," Laura says inferring that she's making a huge sacrifice. She flips open her notebook and writes the date and time.

"Thanks," says Debra.

"Okay," says Jill, looking at her accounting spreadsheet, "from the fifty-fifty we made $68. From the Christmas basket we made, after expenses, $58. And from all the baking, we made $59.25, for a total of $185.25."

"Not bad for a couple of months' work," says Debra.

"Jill," says Steve, "remind me to get that recipe for those date squares from you, honey bun. Those were to-die-for delicious."

"I'll email it to you after the meeting," Jill says, winking.

"Right," says Debra. "How are we going to make some money?"

"We could sell boxes of file folders on the street," I suggest. Everyone laughs.

"You're so naughty, Colin," says Steve.

"How about pizza?" suggests Cindy, almost inaudibly. Cindy is a little mousy girl with a flat chest, thick glasses and horrific fashion sense.

"What's that? I didn't catch what you said, you have to speak up," Debra huffs.

"Pizza, we could sell pizza at lunch," Cindy says a little louder.

"Where could we get pizza from?" Debra asks.

"Um, well actually I was thinking we could get pizza from Gino's down the street," says Cindy. "I already called them and asked them what their best price would be for, say, eight large pizzas, combination, and they told me that they could get me a pizza for twelve dollars. Each one has eight slices. I figure if we sell it at three dollars a slice, we could make twelve dollars a pizza. If we could sell all eight pizzas we would make close to a hundred dollars in profit."

"I love pizza," says Steve, flapping his arms in excitement.

"Good work Cindy," says Laura, scribbling away in her notebook.

"Oh my God," says Jill, bolting up straight in her chair. "I have the perfect way to sell it. Okay, get this, last Halloween I made the best costume for my husband, like ever. He was a giant slice of pizza. I made it out of foam and painted it yellow and glued on these big felt circles for pepperoni. It would be so perfect to sell the pizza."

"Who's going to wear it?" I ask.

All eyes roam back and forth and land back on me. Oh shit.
"Well," says Jill, "it really would only fit Colin. You're about the same size as my husband."

"No way, I'm not dressing up as a giant piece of pizza."

"Oh, Colin, people will love you," says Steve, touching my arm. Then he says to Jill, "Tell me there are tights too! Does Colin get to wear tights?"

"Yep, yellow tights, the colour of cheese."

Steve closes his eyes and vibrates his legs and arms up and down with his fists clenched tight, and makes a high-pitched *eeeeehhhhhh* sound. I guess he's imagining what I would look like in tights. I'm a little disturbed about how excited he's becoming about the whole thing.

"No way," I repeat.

"Please," says Laura. "We'll sell a ton of pizza if you do it. People love you."

"Yes, please Colin," pleads Jill.

"You can't let us down," says Steve.

I look to Debra for some help.

"Sounds like a good marketing gimmick to me," Debra says.

I look to Cindy. Cindy pushes her glasses up her nose and nods her head in agreement with Debra.

"Shit," I say. "Fine, I'll do it."

"That-a-boy Colin," says Steve. "You'll look great in tights, I know it."

"Yeah, great," I say. "Just fabulous."

We decide to sell pizza on Thursday, the day after payday. Jill has given me the costume in a giant black garbage bag, the triangular foam tip poking out the top. There are no change rooms in my building, so I decide to use the handicapped washroom located between the men's and women's washroom just on the other side of my cubicle wall. There's a hook on the back of the door. If you were in a wheelchair, you'd have no hope in reaching this hook and I puzzle why it's there. I hang my pants and peel on the yellow tights. I pull the costume out and wiggle into it. I gaze at myself in the angled-for-a-wheelchair mirror. I look like what I am, a giant six-foot-two slice of pepperoni pizza.

BOOM! The whole wall shakes. What the hell was that? BOOM! It sounds as if somebody's hitting the wall in the men's washroom. It's not a gunshot, so I don't completely panic. They always seem to be doing maintenance in the men's washroom for some reason. But this sounds too loud. I unlock the door and step into the hallway wearing my costume.

"Ahhhhhhhh!" somebody screams, then BOOM! Is somebody being murdered in the men's washroom? Normally the coward in me would run, but curiosity, rather than good conscience, moves me forward toward the door, toward the noise. I see several people's heads are now gophering over their cubicle walls, blatantly disregarding management's policy of not standing on the office furniture. I can see the puzzled looks on their faces, trying to understand the correlation between a giant walking slice of pizza and the incredible booming sounds coming from the washroom. I shrug my shoulders and hold out my hands to let them know I don't have a clue what is going on either, but this gesture is lost on them.

"Nooooooo!" comes another scream, then another BOOM! I'm freaked out. The costume, the foam snug around my head, is giving me claustrophobia. I kick open the washroom door and a billow of smoke wafts out at me in the hall. "Fire!" somebody screams. I hear the muted sounds of shuffling and running feet. I step back into the hallway, letting the door swing shut.

"Ahhhhhhh!" comes the scream again. BOOM! Suddenly the fire alarm goes off. Shit. I kick open the door again, shuffling sideways through the door, the only way I'll fit. I realize that it's not smoke in the air, but plaster dust. BOOM! My heart's racing, my hands perspiring, the hair on the back of my neck raising. Rounding the corner, I spot Barry cowering on the floor between two urinals. His hair and shoulders are covered in plaster dust. He's a frightened animal. There are large holes in the wall above him. I turn a little more, my peripheral vision obscured by the costume, and there's Crazy Larry, naked as the day he was born, holding a sledgehammer. He too is lightly coated in plaster dust, reminding me of Rutger Hauer in *Blade Runner*. His penis looks like a tiny snow-covered yule log.

"The device that is sucking my soul is in the wall," he tells me, not seeming to notice that he is talking to a slice of pizza, just before he swings and BOOM! puts another hole in the wall above Barry's head. Barry whimpers, his lip quivering.

"I know it's in here," says Crazy Larry, swinging again. BOOM! I reach my hand out and Barry grabs hold. I pull at him, but he seems frozen. Crazy Larry doesn't seem to care about us; he just seems to be concerned about the device in the wall that he has manufactured in his warped mind.

"Come on Barry," I yell at him, pulling, "it's time to go!" Finally he moves, following me out the door. BOOM! Crazy Larry screams, "I know it's in here!"

We make our way to the fire-escape door and bolt down the stairs. As we near the bottom flight, two firefighters wearing masks and oxygen tanks on their backs greet us going up. I stop one. "There's no fire, but there's a crazy man putting holes in the wall with a sledgehammer. You need the cops!" I yell over the deafening sounds of the alarm bell.

"Say again?" says one of the firemen.

"No fire, but a crazy man. I wouldn't go up there without a gun!"

The firemen look at each other and the one thumbs back over his shoulder. We all leave the stairwell and head into the ground-floor lobby. Barry's trembling hard. A fireman comes and wraps him in a blanket. When we get outside, hundreds of employees are huddled in groups of three or four, looking up at the building for traces of smoke or flame. Maybe Crazy Larry *will* burn the place down yet, give them something to watch. I tell my story to the chief fireman, and then I tell it again when the cops show up.

"Why are you dressed as a pizza slice?"

"Marketing gimmick to raise money."

"Nice. So, one naked guy with a sledgehammer. Any guns?"

"Not that I'm aware of, but the guy scares the shit out of me. I wouldn't put it past him." It's freezing out, about minus-fifteen Celsius with the wind chill. A lot of my co-workers are crossing the street to Sunshine Valley. I would, too, but apparently they want me to stick around. I end up sitting in the back of a cruiser for a while to warm up. They call in the SWAT team to take down Crazy Larry. They show up within ten minutes, and two media vans pull up, too. A reporter with a camera taps on the window of the car I'm sitting in and asks if I would talk with her. I leave the warmth of the cruiser to carry out an interview about all the exciting commotion that has transpired. I repeat exactly what I'd recited to the cops moments earlier.

Fifteen minutes after the SWAT team goes in, they march back out with Crazy Larry, a bug-eyed zombie, presumably handcuffed underneath the brown blanket his naked form is wrapped in. A couple of photographers are snapping pictures as he's escorted into a police van. I see a bewildered Barry sitting in the back of an ambulance. He seems to have calmed down. I walk over to him. "Colin," he says surprised, as if he hasn't seen me in years, "I don't know what to say. You saved my life."

"I want off the Refrigerator Committee, Barry," I tell him.

"Ah yeah, sure thing," he says.

"Thanks." I walk away and approach a cop to inquire about getting my clothes back. She tells me that the whole area is currently a crime scene, but she'll look into getting them back for me after they finish taking photos. "Shouldn't be more than an hour."

I walk over to the mall and run into Phil outside First Choice Hair Cutters and he nearly pees his pants laughing at my costume. We kill an hour strolling the mall before I head back to get my clothes. I humour a zillion questions from customers asking whether there is a new pizza place opening in the mall, and parents encouraging their kids to have photos taken with me. I do it because I imagine I, too, would want a photo of my Sammy with a slice of pizza.

I head back over to the office building. I'm not allowed to go back into the building because the fire marshal discovered, while inspecting the damage caused by Crazy Larry's hole-punching antics, asbestos in the walls of the men's washroom. They tell me I won't be able to come in for the rest of the week until all the asbestos has been removed and the damage fixed.

I ride the bus home wearing my pizza costume.

At home with Sarah, who can't stop laughing after seeing me on the six o'clock news, the phone rings. It's Barry. He confirms that we will indeed be off for the rest of the week, but should hopefully be returning on Monday.

The next morning I awake to Sarah screaming. Or at least I think it's screaming. Something must have happened to the baby. I yank the covers off and run toward her. She's in the kitchen, laughing, crying, pointing at the newspaper on the kitchen table. I look down. It's the cover of the *Ottawa Sun*, with a picture of Crazy Larry being hauled out in his brown blanket, and me, in costume, standing behind. The headline reads, "A Crazy Slice of Life."

"Beautiful, just fucking beautiful," I say.

Sarah is holding her belly, still laughing.

When I return to work, there is an email informing us that a grief counsellor, Dr. Barnum, has been hired to talk to us about our feelings, about what happened with Crazy Larry. Attendance is highly encouraged. I guess because I was directly involved, I've automatically been scheduled to see Dr. Barnum first thing at 10 a.m. in Boardroom B down the hall.

Dr. Barnum is a large man with thick curly hair and glasses, wearing a well-ironed shirt and purple bowtie. He shakes my hand and asks me to take a seat. So I do. He asks me a series of non-threatening get-to-know-you questions about my job and a little about my personal life: whether I'm married, do I have kids, where did I grow up. This chit-chat goes on for fifteen minutes, then he asks me if I've ever heard of a Rorschach test? I tell him yes and he tells me we should try it. He shows me inkblots and asks me what I see in them.

"Well here and here," I say pointing, "there are clearly two men hiding behind bushes with guns."

"How about this one?"

"In this one a man is stabbing a sheep, that's all the blood pouring out there."

"Okay, and this one?"

"That's a man pushing someone down a hole."

"Interesting," says Dr. Barnum, pushing his glasses up his nose.

"Yes, and look here, the hole has teeth."

Urban Folk Dancers

Sarah and I have been attending prenatal classes in the evenings. This is where a group of pregnant women sit around with their life partners or spouses, and some nurse tells them what's going to happen, what it's like to have a baby. The only reason I agreed to attend is to show Sarah that I'm a dedicated father. The woman who teaches the class is a real hardcore granola. She favours ethnic clothing, usually brightly coloured ponchos or East Indian patterned shirts with wooden beaded necklaces. Apparently she has four children, but she is unattractive with a personality to match, not even a sense of humour to save her.

Last week Sarah and I were joking around on the birthing ball. We were supposed to be practising different positions, all the while performing the appropriate breathing techniques while we worked through pretend contractions. Sarah was on her knees hugging the ball, as were all the women in the class, and the men were behind rubbing the ladies' backs. I made some remark about how I thought this position is how we got into this class in the first place. The couple beside us, with whom we've made friends, laughed. Miss whole-grain loaf came over and said, "Humour will only get you so far in the delivery room." What a delightful woman.

This week's class is going to be on episiotomies and circumcision. Since we know we're having a girl, and since it's Phil's birthday, I begged Sarah to give this class a skip. She said she wanted to go anyway, just in case we had a boy for our second child, but I was free to take the night off. I was going to suggest that we see how the first child goes before we consider having a second. But then I thought better of it and kept my mouth shut.

I meet Phil and a couple of buddies he went to school with, Roy and Ross, at The Keg for dinner down in the market. His friends appear to be good guys and we get along just fine. Phil tells the story of Crazy Larry and the pizza costume and has them in stitches. We drink a lot of beer and each of us buys Phil a shot. After, we go to a dance club so Phil can check out the ladies. I ask him where the hell Zoe is. He says that he told her he needed a guy's night out. She's apparently giving him something very special for his birthday tomorrow, he tells me with a big drunken smile plastered across his face. I refrain from inquiring. The club is dead because we are too early. So we head over to the Chateau Lafayette for a couple pints. I'm getting pretty drunk and I keep calling Ross, Roy and Roy, Ross. One of them suggests that we should hit the urban folk dancers.

"Urban folk dancers, what are they?" I ask.

"Dude," says Phil, "the peelers, across the street at the Barefax."

"Jesus, Sarah will have my balls. I'm supposed to be at a prenatal class."

"Don't tell her," says Ross, or is it Roy?

"Yeah, let's go," says the other one.

The music is loud and the light is dim and everything seems to be accented in neon trim, pink and blue. A man the size of a vending machine with a bald head and a handlebar moustache reminiscent of the one Sarah's great-grandfather has in the picture in our hallway watches us expressionlessly as we make our way through the coat check and into the bar. There's a woman on stage wearing nothing but thigh-high white boots. She's bent over, palms pressed flat against the stage, showing the men in perverts' row that no, she has never undergone an episiotomy, all to the musical offerings of Finger Eleven. The place is not that busy so we get a good table with a clear view of the stage. I order a beer and end up paying eight bucks for it, including tip. The next thing I know, we have tequila shots lined up all over the table and Roy and Ross have hired a sassy redhead to table-dance for us. Now, I consider myself a devoted and loyal husband, but as a male still in my prime, I can't help but imagine what taking this little firecracker to bed would involve: screaming, the clawing of bedsheets, a virtuoso performance. Wow! Having sex with Sarah, now that she is pregnant, is a little odd for me. It's not that the sex is bad; it's just that when we're having it, I keep flashing to an ultrasound image of Sammy being poked in the eye socket by the head of my penis. It's an awful image. Now here I am, looking at this fine specimen of womanhood, and that's what I'm thinking about, Sammy getting poked in the womb by her father's dick.

"Drink up," says Phil, passing me some sort of purple shooter. I drink it, thinking I probably shouldn't. I look around the room at the other men. There are a couple of guys at the next table who appear to be bikers. I'm sure they supply these girls with cocaine or whatever they need. Ross stands up and knocks over one of the biker's beers on a trip to the washroom, but is too drunk to notice. The biker stands up and grabs Ross by the shirt collar and spins him around. Ross sees who he's dealing with and babbles out a series of apologies. We placate the whole situation by buying the two of them a new round of drinks and a table dance. My heart is still moving faster than it should be. I'm still riding a wave of adrenalin. What if the guy had a knife; what if things had escalated? I think of the head-line, "Bar Fight Turns Tragic." I picture Sarah telling Sammy that her father died in a strip club. "Guys, I've got to go home soon," I tell them.

Outside I bum a smoke off Roy. I'm one of those drunken smokers, the kind real smokers hate. I cough and hack my way through it as we all tumble back to the dance bar. Within twenty minutes, Phil hooks up with some attractive blonde and Ross seems to be doing well with her friend. I yell over the music to Roy that I'm going to take off. He nods his head, not really giving a shit either way. I think about saying goodbye to Phil, but I don't want to interrupt his gyration on the dance floor.

I stagger to the local poutine stand and get myself a large. I catch a cab and eat it in the backseat on the way home. I ask the cabbie the time and he tells me it's a quarter to two. Shit, I hope Sarah is in bed. The motion of the cab is making me queasy. I can't eat anymore. Feeling wonky. Don't get sick in the cab. Don't get sick in the cab. I chant this mantra to myself until I arrive safely home.

The light is on when I come in the door. I hope I'm not go-ing to get the why-didn't-you-call lecture. I told Sarah I was going to be late. I told her not to wait up. She comes barrelling out into the hallway to greet me. "You went to a strip club?!" screams Sarah.

How the hell could she know that? "How the hell do you know that?" I ask.

"You sack of shit, I can't believe you went to see strippers!"

"Listen, it wasn't my idea. I was there, but I decided I didn't want to be knifed in a strip club. I've vowed never to go back."

Sarah comes closer to me, then jerks her head back like she has discovered a mouldy container of food in the refrigerator. "You stink. Were you smoking?"

"Yes, I had a cigarette. What's the big deal? How did you know I was at the strip club?"

"I checked our online banking and you debited forty dollars at the club."

"Well aren't you a clever one, Miss CSI."

"Fuck you Colin, you…"

I take off running to the toilet. I manage to make it just in time. Sarah screams from the doorway, "Are you committed to this baby or are you committed to drinking fucking beer with Phil? I swear to God Colin, if you don't improve your behaviour, if you don't lay off the booze, I'll get a fucking abortion! I'm not living this way."

"Jesus," I moan, hugging the toilet, "can you give me a little break here. Besides, isn't it a bit late for an abortion?"

"Bastard!" she yells, slamming the washroom door. A few seconds later, I hear the bedroom door slam. I manage to clean myself up, rinse my mouth out, and then lurch over to the living room couch, turning out the light on the way. I promptly collapse.

I'm almost asleep when Sarah comes charging back out, snapping the light back on. "I swear to you Colin, if you don't commit to this baby, I'll leave you," she says.

"I'm fucking committed. Jesus, turn out the light will you? Enough already."

"Turn it out yourself!" she yells, turning around, marching back to bed. SLAM! goes the bedroom door again.

Christ almighty.

The next day, I call in sick to work. I spend the day recovering. I do penance by cleaning our apartment head to toe, and making Sarah a homemade spaghetti and meatball dinner, each meatball hand-rolled with love. I limit myself to one glass of wine with dinner. We drive over after dinner to Elgin Street and go to the Mayflower restaurant for coconut cream pie and decaffeinated coffees.

She hasn't brought it up since she left for work this morning. "So tell me," she says, shovelling a big piece of pie into her face, "were the girls attractive? Did you get a boner?"

"Yes they were, and no I did not."

"Why, are you gay, or you just can't get it up when you're drunk?"

"Very funny. Are you done with this?"

"Are you sorry?"

"Very sorry."

"I'm done."

Mr. Peaches

Today we celebrated Peter Cann's retirement luncheon in the big boardroom. There were speeches, gifts, balloons, tons of food and a spectacular slideshow that Phil had put together with pictures of Peter superimposed on various and easily recognizable world monuments, places that Peter said he will travel to when he retired – Peter at the Eiffel Tower, Peter at the Egyptian Pyramids, Peter in lederhosen on the side of a mountain looking at a goat; the next slide Peter is in bed with the goat. This kind of risqué push of the political correctness envelope, in our uptight office seems to go over surprisingly well, even with upper management. Maybe somebody spiked the punch, or maybe people were still a little on edge after Crazy Larry and the asbestos aftermath and really just needed a good cathartic laugh. Whatever the reason, it was actually kind of fun.

I'm disappointed that Peter is leaving. Aside from Phil, Peter was the one beacon of light in a sea of watered-down bean counters. People here are as intellectually appetizing as a bowl of melted vanilla ice cream. Which reminds me, Bruce has now worked up the courage to speak to me directly again. He told me at the luncheon that they'd found a replacement for Brita. Apparently after Crazy Larry did his thing, some manager noticed that we actually had a handicapped washroom, but we had no disabled person to use it. For some reason somebody somewhere thought that the washroom needed justification. We were lagging in some sort of quota, hence we needed to get a cripple, as Bruce put it. So, we are getting Jackie. Jackie is not in a wheelchair. Jackie is blind. Supposedly she is legally blind, but not a hundred percent blind. She does have some very limited tunnel vision. "She's starting tomorrow," Bruce tells me. "You can show her the ropes."

In advance of her arrival, two tech maintenance people come in and replace Brita's computer and monitor with some interesting-looking equipment. Jackie's monitor is huge. Attached on its corner is a swivel arm with a giant round magnifying glass. Her keyboard has Braille bumps on the keys. They load interactive speech software to enable Jackie to talk to her PC. They also install a Braille printer on her desk. So much for Paperless Office.

I'm working away, lost in some tricky code, when I hear Bruce clear his throat behind me. I spin in my chair and there's Bruce and a woman who's about forty-five, wearing a horrific purple and yellow paisley dress. She's smiling yet not looking at me, but rather just above me and slightly to the right. In her hand she's clutching the handle of a harness fastened to a panting golden retriever.

"Colin, I would like you to meet Jackie and Mr. Peaches, the guide dog."

"Pleased to meet you," says Jackie, extending her arm out into the air.

I stand and take her hand, touching her slightly on the arm to correct her position so she's facing me and not my cubicle wall.

"Nice to meet you."

"Colin here will be showing you the ropes. Get you going. Here's her user ID and temporary passcode," says Bruce, passing me a piece of paper. When I reach for it, I notice Carla. She has turned in her seat and is looking at Mr. Peaches, horrified. Bruce catches my glance. "Oh," he says. "Almost forgot, your other cubicle partner here is Carla."

Jackie turns, following Bruce's voice and faces Carla. "Pleased to meet you," she says, again extending her hand into the air.

Carla doesn't move. This is interesting; nobody has ever tried to shake Carla's hand before. I see one of my co-workers, Jill from the Refrigerator Committee, in the hallway heading to the washroom. She sees the situation. Jill is bright. She pivots and slides gracefully past Bruce so she is now facing Jackie. She takes her hand and says, "Pleased to meet you too." Then she slips back into the hallway and is gone. Jackie looks puzzled as to why her co-worker came and left from the direction of the hall. I throw Jill a smile and a thumbs-up for her brilliant miniscule charade. She winks back and wanders off.

Bruce steers a confused-looking Jackie away from a confused-looking Carla and says, "And this is where you'll be sitting."

"Where's Dan?" I ask Bruce. I haven't seen the guy in at least a week.

"Dan's been diagnosed with fibromyalgia. I don't think he'll be back. I've been meaning to come and talk to you about this. Until we can find a replacement, you'll need to take over for Dan."

This comes as no surprise. It won't make much difference since I'm doing 95 percent of his work anyway. I think Dan knew in his heart that he would end up on long-term disability. My heart knew it, too. "No worries, Bruce, I've got it covered."

"Jackie here is going to be working on updating the threshold conversion document. So if you can show her what she needs to do, that'll be great."

Updating the threshold conversion document is about as useful a task as counting grains of sand on a beach – useless and never-ending. Brita never did it for just that reason. I assume Bruce has given her this task because it doesn't matter if she screws it up or not; nobody ever looks at it. So now, on top of doing my own work, Brita's work, and Dan's work, I have to babysit Jackie and Mr. Peaches. Great.

I spend the rest of the afternoon trying to get Jackie logged onto the mainframe. The LAN people give her the word "password" to temporarily log in with, and she manages to lock herself out by incorrectly typing it. We have to call and get it reset, three times. Turns out she had caps lock turned on. Jackie is extremely slow. Watching her trying to perceive what's happening on the screen with the giant fish-eye lens is comically painful. It's even difficult for me to navigate the screen because everything is enormous. Even if Jackie could see, it's still a nightmare trying to manoeuvre around the LAN to find any document; everything seems to be buried six file folders deep. I spend the next two days just trying to get her set up. I am the Miracle Worker.

A week has gone by. Sarah has pain in her lower back and isn't sleeping well. Hence I'm not sleeping well either. I'm washing my hands in the bathroom sink at work. My thoughts float around my mind like a mobile: Is my book scary enough? What if Sammy hates me? Did I forget to take out the garbage? Why do I think about these things? Can I think any differently than I do? Why do I keep thinking about what I'm thinking about?

I look at myself in the mirror. Bloodshot eyes look back. Dope-smoking eyes. Maybe it's pinkeye? Maybe it's eye cancer? A wave of panic washes over me. I clutch the counter. My heart is galloping. Maybe I'm having a heart attack? When I finally calm down and am able to compose myself, I walk over and tell Bruce that I have to go to the doctor. At the clinic there is a forty-five-minute wait. What if they have to remove both my eyes and I'll never get to see Sammy before she is born? What if I die? Sammy will never get to know her father. I'll have to make videos for all of her birthdays until she turns twenty-one. The last one will be me in Randy Pausch style expelling nuggets of wisdom: follow your passion Sammy, don't settle for an office job, you'll hate yourself and end up dying of eye cancer.

"Colin MacDonald?" chimes a voice.

An unfriendly nurse brings me to a little room to wait for the doctor. I stare at the poster on the wall, a cross-section of the middle ear. Maybe I'll go deaf too? Then there's a knock and the door opens. A little East Indian woman enters with a clipboard and introduces herself as Dr. Lakhani. She tells me it's probably just allergies and sends me down the street for tests. Turns out I'm allergic to dogs. Maybe I should adopt a few pieces from Carla's new wardrobe. She's taken to wearing a white lab coat, rubber surgical gloves and an air-filtering mask. A rash has formed on Carla's cheek around the edge of the mask. She looks as if she should be working in a laboratory for infectious diseases. It turns out I am the one who could probably use the mask.

I'm the last to arrive at our weekly group meeting, which now, after the loss of Dan and Brita, consists of Bruce, Carla, myself, Jackie and Mr. Peaches. Bruce is going over a meeting he had with the managers about the sense of urgency and the need for commitment from every employee to reach the goal of Paperless Office 2012. I smell shit. No, it's not what's coming from Bruce's mouth, I mean I smell real shit. I look over and there in the corner of the room, next to the easel with the large sheets of paper used for brainstorming (in most cases it's a light drizzle), is Mr. Peaches, taking a dump on the carpet. "Bruce, check it out," I say pointing, interrupting him.

"Oh my. Jackie, Mr. Peaches seems to be going to the washroom."

"Mr. Peaches!" cries Jackie. "Bad dog, bad dog. Come over here." The dog looks sullen. It slowly comes over and lies down next to Jackie's chair.

"Colin, would you mind cleaning that up?" asks Bruce casually, as if he were asking me to retrieve a pen that had fallen on the floor. I'm surprised he has the nerve to ask after he has only recently recovered from fearing for his own physical safety.

"Yeah I mind," I say.

"I'll get it, just show me where it is," Jackie says.

"Why doesn't Carla get it, she's wearing gloves?" I suggest. I can't really read Carla's expression because of the mask.

"Colin, please, we can't leave it there," says Bruce.

"You pick it up then," I tell him.

"Why is Carla wearing gloves?" asks Jackie.

"Fine, I need to get a baggy," says Bruce.

"I always carry baggies in my purse," says Jackie. "I'll go to my desk and get one."

"I'll get it for you Jackie," I say.

"Oh, thanks Colin. My purse is in my desk drawer," she tells me.

In my lengthy chats with Jackie, I've discovered a few things about Mr. Peaches. Jackie, because she does have some limited vision, wasn't on the top of the list to receive a dog. But Mr. Peaches came along because he flunked out of seeing-eye-dog school from the States. Apparently he barks at pigs. I'm not sure if that's enough to get you flunked, or if he lacks in some other capacity. I do know that when Jackie takes his harness off there is no evidence of any special abilities. She usually takes his harness off for most of the day. Mr. Peaches runs all over the office. I walked into my director's office the other day and low and behold, there was Mr. Peaches sniffing her crotch. Charming.

On my way back to my cube I catch glimpses of other people's garbage cans. They're overflowing. Rose and Jessica, the two African ladies who clean our offices, are terrified of Mr. Peaches and have basically stopped cleaning our floor. They only work during the day, so the garbage hasn't been picked up for over a week now. I find the baggy in Jackie's purse and bring it back to our meeting. I pass it to Bruce. I ask him as he's scooping, "So what's the time code for picking up crap, Bruce? Does that go under general maintenance?"

After the meeting is over, I'm extremely itchy everywhere, like I'm wearing wool pyjamas. I have red blotches which I imagine are hives. Mr. Peaches is sending me over the edge. But then something happens. Determinism. Some people call it fate. Was it always going to unfold this way? Yes. Somebody had the idea that the hundreds of boxes of file folders in the coffee room were taking up too much room. Could they have thought any differently? So they stacked them up to the ceiling. Here's an interesting fact you might enjoy: Ottawa is built on a fault line. From time to time, the good people of Ottawa experience a rumble: not just a cabinet shuffle in Parliament, but a real live earthquake. As fate would have it, Jackie and Mr. Peaches went to the coffee room in search of a cup when the earthquake struck. A ten-foot wall of boxes, each box being of substantial size and weight, came crashing down atop Jackie and Mr. Peaches. Jackie was rushed to the hospital where they determined that she had a concussion and a broken collarbone. Mr. Peaches went to the vet where they determined he had a broken front leg.

The next day, all the garbage is picked up, my hives are gone and my eyes aren't as red anymore. I receive an email from management saying that due to the hazardous situation in the coffee room, everyone will be required to store two boxes of file folders at his or her desk for the time being. Dr. Barnum would be available if anyone desired to talk about their feelings concerning what happened to Jackie and Mr. Peaches. Later in the day, I get an envelope dropped off in my in-basket containing two get-well-soon cards, one for Jackie and one for Mr. Peaches, and a little pouch for donations for a gift. I sign both cards thinking why, because she is never going to see it anyway. I slip a toonie into the pouch and then put the envelope into Carla's in-basket. A maintenance guy comes by with a cart and drops two boxes of file folders in each cubicle of our quad. After he leaves, I move my boxes to Jackie's cube. She and Mr. Peaches are going to be off work for quite some time.

Three months later…

From the Hole Emerges Life

The last three months have been hectic. Sarah's up every hour to pee and her back is killing her. Sammy's been kicking non-stop. Apparently she never stops moving. Well actually, she did last month. Sarah called me at work and said she hadn't felt Sammy move since one o'clock. It was 2:30 when she called. I told her to relax, that she'd be fine, just give it some more time. We, of course, ended up in emergency at the Civic Hospital sitting around the waiting room for three hours, only to discover that everything was perfectly normal. Sammy began to kick away madly when the nurse put the heart monitor on Sarah's belly.

I've been sleeping on the couch the past few nights because Sarah is up all the time. She's ten days overdue. We're going to the hospital today so she can be induced. So hopefully, I'll be seeing little Sammy soon. The car seat has been installed and the hospital bag was packed three weeks ago: a couple of pairs of pyjamas for Sarah, her bathrobe, toiletries, infant diapers, a baby blanket, an outfit for Sammy to wear home, and the video camera with extra tapes and batteries. When we pull into the parking lot, which is still under construction, Sarah blurts out that she is scared.

"What are you worried about?"

"What if something happens?" she asks, squeezing my hand.

"Listen, whatever happens, happens. But this is a good hospital with very knowledgeable doctors and nurses. They have all the fancy equipment in case anything should happen, which it won't."

"How can you be sure? What if the cord wraps around her neck? I think about that all the time, Sammy being strangled by the cord," Sarah says, grabbing her belly.

"What is it?" I ask, because I can tell by the look on her face that something is wrong.

"Nothing, I just haven't felt her move in a while."

"When's a while?"

"Just a second," she says pushing on her belly with the palm of her hand.

"When? When's the last time you felt her move?"

"Maybe an hour ago."

"Jesus, let's go."

The round suction-cup end of the video camera's viewfinder rests against my eye socket as the word "REC" flashes in red in the upper right hand corner of my visual screen. "Tell us what's going on," I ask Sarah who's sitting in a lavender hospital chair with two straps around her torso monitoring Sammy's heart-beat and her own possible contractions.

"Jesus, Colin, do you have to film this?"

"Hey, Sammy's going to love this when she's older."

"I don't want all this on film."

"Why not?"

"Fine. Film away," she says, looking away from the camera at the wall.

"Sarah has just had the insert placed into her cervix to soften it and hopefully this will get things moving along. Sarah is being monitored in case of uterine hyperstimulation, which means she would have contractions right away. Nothing is happening at the moment." I pan over to the monitoring equipment, then pan back to Sarah and zoom in on her face.

"Can you turn that shit off?" she asks.

After forty minutes of nothing, they send us home. We stop for lunch at the hospital cafeteria because Sarah is starving. She orders a cheeseburger and fries with gravy, but manages only to eat half before she says she's full. Her stomach is being squished by Sammy sitting on it. I anticipated this, so I only bought a small salad.

As soon as we get in the door, Sarah rushes to the washroom to pee. "Colin, it fell out!" she yells calmly.

"What, the insert or the baby?"

"Very funny. The insert. What should we do?"

I call the hospital and they tell us to come back in. So back we go. A different doctor comes in and reinserts the insert. "There, that ought to do it," she says. We head back home.

"I'm having pain," says Sarah on the way home in the car.

"Are you okay, should I turn around?"

"No, no. They said there might be a little discomfort associated with the insert. I should be fine."

When we arrive back home for the second time, Sarah seems quite uncomfortable. "I don't know Colin, it seems really intense, cramping. I'm going to take a bath to see if it takes the edge off." She does this for a while, then she says, "Jesus, maybe the first time when they monitored us it wasn't in. Then they put it in properly and they didn't monitor us. You know, Colin, I think I'm having contractions here. Phone the hospital!"

I phone and they tell me to tell Sarah to take the insert out. So I do and she does. She gets out of the bath and gets dressed and we drive back to the hospital. When we hit the maternity ward, Sarah is writhing in pain. We are taken to a room where a doctor can check her out. She gets undressed again and puts on a green hospital gown which is open all down the back. As soon as she sits down on the examination table, there is a small almost-inaudible pop. "Something happened, I'm all wet," Sarah says. I can tell she is doing her best to stay calm.

"Relax honey," says one of the nurses. "Your water broke is all."

Sarah looks scared. I have no clue what to expect. I too sometimes think about the cord wrapping around little Sammy's neck, but I'd never tell Sarah that. "You're fine baby," I tell her in the most soothing voice I can muster. "You're going to do great."

The doctor checks her and tells her everything is fine, tells Sarah to relax. After they put a plastic IV lock in her hand, they take us to a birthing room. She's contracting every minute. She's been hyperstimulated. She went from zero to sixty, full-on contractions, in a matter of minutes when they put the insert in the second time. When we get to the birthing room, I'm surprised at how big it is. In fact it's enormous. Sarah's become wild, her eyes have widened and her breathing is rapid. "I can't get on top of the pain. I'm so hot," she says ripping her hospital gown from her body. She's running around in a circle clutching her lower back, her head flopping, spinning as she moans in pain. I look to the nurse for help.

"Okay, Sarah sweetie," says the nurse, "you need to calm down."

"Okay," says Sarah, slowing her pace but continuing to walk around the room.

"Would you like something to ease the pain?"

"Yes," she blurts.

"Would you like to try the Jacuzzi tub?"

"Sure, but something for the pain." I help Sarah get into the tub and get the bubbles going while the nurse leaves to get some drug called Nubain.

"I'm sorry Colin, I wanted to do it without the drugs, but I didn't think the pain would be this intense. It just came on so fast. I think I'm going to need to take the epidural."

"It's okay, baby," I tell her. "You're doing great. You just hang in there."

I run the water in the tub and get the jets going. I help Sarah in. She flops around the tub like a whale. She's moaning in pain.

"Oh God, I'm going to be sick," she says.

I help her out of the tub and Sarah throws up, missing the toilet of course. Most of it hits the side of the Jacuzzi.

"Sorry," she says.

"Don't worry about it."

"I have to go to the washroom," she says, sitting down on the toilet.

"You do that."

The nurse comes in and sees the vomit.

"Oh, a little accident. Don't worry, we'll get that cleaned up. I've got your Nubain when you're finished."

The drug doesn't do much for Sarah and she's in a state of

panic. She orders the epidural. After a gut-wrenching two-hour wait of watching Sarah in agony, the anaesthesiologist finally comes and gives her the epidural. After this Sarah can't walk, she's numb from the waist down. But now she's comfortable. When she lies back in bed, the muscles in her shoulders, neck and face relax. I relax, too. I didn't realize how wound up I'd become. Watching Sarah go through that kind of pain, it was like hundreds of little strings were being pulled all over my body, making various parts of my body involuntarily contract. Women say men don't understand the pain of childbirth. Maybe so. I'll never know it, but I have a vivid imagination and a stockpile of empathy.

Before the epidural I'd been watching *The Exorcist* and suddenly the channel changed to *The Sound of Music*. Now it's all birds and butterflies. Sarah is smiling. She asks me to pass her *People* magazine. I realize that I'm super hungry. It's almost nine and we haven't eaten anything since lunch. Sarah isn't allowed to eat anything but clear fluids and Jell-O. They don't want Sarah vomiting while she is anesthetized and choking to death on a cafeteria cheeseburger. "Listen babe, do you mind if I go grab a bite to eat?"

"Sure honey, just be a sweetie pie and get me a ginger ale before you go."

My wife is five floors up, paralyzed from the waist down, about to birth out my first child and I'm staring at the cafeteria salad bar. Guilt hangs about my mind, a crooked shadow in my skull; I should be feeling more. This is a life-pivoting moment, but here I am, thinking about my stomach. Maybe I'll be a rotten father? Profound thoughts or feelings about my situation aside, a man has to eat.

The mushrooms, the broccoli, the olives, the carrots, all the veggies for that matter, look like they have let out a collective sigh, and they each lie existentially defeated in small round beige containers surrounded by crushed ice. Blue cheese, French and Italian dressings languish to one side. I decide to skip the healthy choice for fear of being depressed. I move to the main food counter. A little gruff woman dressed in a white kitchen uniform and a hairnet barks that the daily special is cabbage rolls. She uncovers a rectangular silver tray containing their grey leafy bodies resting in a red sauce which I imagine should be tangy, but it's probably as bland as paste.

"I think I'll just get a cheeseburger," I tell her. She seems pissed.

"Lettuce, onion, tomato, pickle?" she rattles at me at high speed.

"Yeah, sure, the works."

"Fries?" she spits.

"Sure."

"Gravy?" she yells.

"No thanks." Jesus, what's with this lady?

I watch as she fries a pre-cooked patty and places not just depressed veggies, but suicidal ones on my hamburger bun. The slice of tomato looks like it has reached the end. The crinkly fries have been under the heat lamp since 8 a.m., I'm sure. She passes me my platter and says, "Enjoy," without a smile.

I don't want to eat in front of Sarah, so I grab a seat and quickly try to wolf it down, worried too that I might be needed upstairs. The cheeseburger has a strange chemical taste to it, as do the fries. I pour ketchup over everything but it still tastes like what it is, bad hospital cafeteria food. I manage to eat half of it and give up. When I get back up to our room, Sarah is still reading her magazine.

"Hi honey, would you be a sweetie pie and get me some Jell-O and ginger ale?" she asks again.

For the next twelve hours we ride out the storm of labour. There's a chair for me that unfolds into an uncomfortable makeshift bed. We both drift in and out, trying to sleep, trying to stay comfortable. But the excitement, the worry, keeps both of us up. Every once in a while I pull out the video camera and take some footage, noting the time and how many centimetres Sarah is dilated.

At 8:42 in the morning, Sarah's reached ten centimetres – show time. The doctor comes into the room with several other people. I'm filming and holding Sarah's hand.

"I'm scared," Sarah repeats again to me.

"You're doing fine," I tell her trying to channel the soothing voice our hippie prenatal instructor said I should be using.

"Okay, when you feel a contraction I want you to push for the duration of the contraction," says the nurse.

Sarah pushes with each contraction. "I can't do it," she says.

"Yes you can," the nurse reassures her.

"I can't. I'm telling you I can't"

"You can. You have to."

"Aaagrrrrrraahhhhh!"

"Good, that's it."

"Aaahhhhherrga!"

"Good, good"

This continues for twenty minutes, and then I see the top of Sammy's head appear, and then disappear in a kind of peek-a-boo game being played out with Sarah's vagina. Then in one screaming giant push Sammy's head pops out. It's a light shade of purple. Her eyes are closed and she appears not to be breathing. I think, stillborn. Maybe she was strangled by the cord? I panic. I look around the room at the faces of the doctors and nurses. I scan them for any signs, a look of horror or panic on their faces, something to confirm my fear that yes, Sammy is dead. Nothing. Then Sarah performs yet another mighty push and Sammy's shoulders come through. Then the rest of her seems to slip out. I see movement!

"She's alive!" I yell. Perhaps it's the lack of sleep, or our long struggle to have a child, but a furnace door opens inside me, a heat that radiates from my navel to my head and it comes out of my body as hot tears. Somebody asks me if I want to cut the cord. I do, first wiping my face on my shirt sleeves.

"Is she healthy?" Sarah asks, trying to see.

"She's beautiful, baby, beautiful."

"I did it," Sarah says.

"Yes, yes you did, baby."

I call my mother and she's crazy excited. She tells me she's on her way to the hospital to meet Sammy. Then I debate who to call next, my father or Sarah's mother. I call Sarah's mother, not really sure which is the lesser of two evils.

"Hello, Franklin residence," says a cold voice. It's Sarah's mother.

"Hello Barbara, it's me, Colin. Your granddaughter was just born."

"Oh great. Everything went smoothly I take it?" she says with almost no enthusiasm in her voice, as if I just told her I replaced an air filter in her car.

"Fairly smoothly I guess you could say."

"Do you still plan on naming the child Samantha?"

"Yes, but I think we're going to call her Sammy."

Silence.

"Hello?" I say.

"Yes Colin, I'll be up in a couple of days as we discussed to help out."

"Sounds good."

"Give my best to Sarah."

"Will do."

"Goodbye Colin."

"Bye, Barbara." I hang up. What a bitch.

I call over to my father's house. His wife answers. She tells me he left for the hospital a while ago. Just as I hang up I hear, "Hey Tiger." My father hasn't called me Tiger since I was eight. I spin around. "Dad?"

There's my father, flowers in one hand and a box in the other. "Where's that granddaughter of mine?" he asks, booze coming off his breath.

"How did you know to come to the hospital?"

"She was scheduled to have the induction yesterday, wasn't she?"

"You remembered that?"

"Had it circled on the calendar. When there was no answer at your place last night, I figure you must be in here. I came down this morning at six."

"You've been here since six?"

"Brought a little something to nip on," he says, pulling a silver flask from his pocket. "Want a nip?"

"No thanks."

"Here you go," he says passing me a box of cigars. "I put little pink bands around each of them. They're Dominican. I took a couple for myself. They're damn good. Pass 'em out to all your friends."

"Gee, thanks Dad."

"No problem, now let's see this Sammy girl." Despite the fact that my father has been drinking since six in the morning, he's good company and leaves shortly after seeing Sarah and the baby. He says he'll swing by tomorrow. As he leaves, I see my mother coming down the hallway with balloons and flowers and another stuffed creature – a yellow duck.

"Hi Mom."

"Oh baby, give me a big hug!" she yells, wrapping herself around me.

"Where are they?" she asks.

"Follow me Mom, this way."

Pushed Over the Edge

Sarah's breasts are enormous. They were big before, but now they are triple-X porn-star boobs. She's having a heck of a time trying to get Sammy to latch. Imagine trying to suck on a spring roll that was attached to the Goodyear Blimp – you get the idea? Sarah's solution has been to dribble colostrum, the pre-milk, from her breasts into Sammy's mouth, as if she were a baby bird.

The first night at home goes fairly smoothly, I think. Sammy's sleeping in our room in an antique bassinet beside our bed. Sarah slept in this thing when she was a baby, as did Barbara. Sammy sleeps for five hours straight. I don't sleep well because Sarah's perched like a gargoyle at the side of the bassinet, making sure that Sammy is breathing. I try to get her to relax, but she can't. At 2 a.m. Sammy wakes up screaming. She has peed through her diaper. I get a cloth and change everything. I record the urination on a yellow card that the hospital gave us, which we have to give to our doctor in few days. Sarah then tries to feed her but can't get the latch, so Sarah does the dribble. Sammy drinks down an ounce. "Want to try and burp her?" asks Sarah.

"Sure."

She passes me Sammy and I balance her on my knee. I hold her bobble-head with thumb and index fingers, squishing her chubby cheeks, palm supporting her chest as I gently tap her on the back with the palm of my other hand. Sammy lets out a significant belch. Sarah and I smile.

"Isn't she the cutest?" Sarah asks.

"Yeah, pretty cute."

"I love you, Colin."

"Love you too, baby."

Sarah begins to cry.

"You okay?" I ask.

"Just tired and happy."

"Me too," I say, rocking Sammy in my arms. "Me too."

Barbara arrives from Toronto the next day. I greet her at the door with Sammy in my arm. She peers at Sammy as if she were selecting which Rolex was the most expensive in the showcase.

"What do you think of your granddaughter?"

"Quite lovely."

"Would you like to hold her?"

She looks at me like I'm offering her a haul off a crack pipe. "Uh, sure," she says, taking Sammy into her arms. I swear I'll never understand how this lady managed to raise children.

Sarah comes out of the washroom and sees her mother holding Sammy. "Oh Mom isn't she adorable?" asks Sarah, flying to her mother's side.

"Colin, would you mind getting my bags? They're in the

car," Barbara says, extending her keys. Barbara doesn't ask, she orders.

"Sure thing," I say. As soon as I get outside a weight lifts; somebody has taken their foot off my chest. The mother-in-law tension has already begun. Barbara thinks Sarah could have done a whole lot better than marry a government bureaucrat wannabe writer. Barbara wishes I had aspired to be something to help her be socially triumphant during her gin rummy games with her affluent friends: my son-in-law is a brain surgeon or my son-in-law is a corporate lawyer.

Sarah told me that her father had met another woman, but before he could leave Barbara he died of cancer. Subsequently, there was no divorce scandal and the pristine veneer of country clubs and church socials remained firmly intact. Barbara's been playing the role of grieving widow for over ten years now. What surprises me is that Sarah puts up with the charade of mourning. I wonder if I can sneak off to the bar for a drink?

I pop the trunk of Barbara's Audi, grab all four bags, which are as heavy as Sarah's childhood guilt. I drag the lot back inside and into the living room. In Sammy's room I've set up a $250 cot – Barbara wouldn't sleep on anything less according to Sarah.

"Oh, Colin, you brought everything in. You can put those two back," orders Barbara, pointing at the two bigger bags.

"Oh, what are these for?" I ask.

"Those are my clothes, those two are gifts for Sarah and the baby."

"Clothes? Don't you want me to put them in your room?"

"Room?"

"Yeah, we got a cot set up in Sammy's room for you."

"Oh no, I'm staying at the Westin, dear."

I put the bags back in the car. I wonder if I can return the cot? I'm fuming. Back inside, Barbara says, "Colin, would you be a dear and get me a few things at the store?"

"What do you need, Barb?"

Sarah can tell I'm pissed and is giving me the look of death.

"I need a bottle of Absolut vodka, cranberry juice, ice – unless you have lots in the freezer. And can you also get soda crackers and some good cheese."

She pulls a hundred from her purse and remains seated, holding out the bill. I walk over and snatch the bill. Barbara reaches into her purse and pulls out a pack of menthol cigarettes.

"Barb, you can't smoke around the baby," I tell her.

She looks to Sarah.

"Mom, really, you'll have to go outside."

Barbara sighs and says, "Fine," and puts the package back in her handbag. Barbara reminds me of Mrs. Robinson from *The Graduate*.

When I get back, I fix drinks for Barbara and me, and then move on to dinner. I'm making Sarah her favourite, spaghetti and meatballs. I mix the ground beef with an egg, breadcrumbs, freshly grated parmesan cheese and parsley. I hand-roll forty tiny meatballs, which I'm frying when the doorbell rings. Sarah is trying to breastfeed and Barbara is outside smoking. I run to the door. It's the public health nurse. She asks how things are going. I tell her fine, but explain that Sammy's having trouble latching. She jumps in and immediately helps Sarah get repositioned. The doorbell rings again. Barbara's locked herself out. The phone rings. I run and answer it. It's my mother, asking how it's going. I tell her it's busy and whisper that Barbara is driving me nuts. She tells me that Great Uncle Lester died the other day at ninety-two. I haven't seen Uncle Lester since I was six. I interrupt her and ask if I can call her back. I put the phone down and it immediately rings again. "Hello?"

"Is this Colin MacDonald?"

"Yes?"

"I'm calling to…"

"No thanks," I say slamming down the phone.

The smoke alarm goes off. The fucking meatballs! I run to the kitchen, which is full of smoke. Sammy is screaming. I pull the pan off the stove and throw it into the sink, open the window, grab a chair and stand on it to pull out the battery from the alarm. Barbara waltzes into the kitchen waving the air, coughing ever so slightly and looks at the charred marbles in the sink. "Well that's not very good now, is it? Maybe we should do take-out. Do you know any Thai places that deliver?" asks Barbara.

After dinner I clean up all the tinfoil trays and wash the dishes. Sarah comes up to me and says, "Why don't you take the laptop and go out for a bit, do some writing? You haven't written in several days."

"Are you sure? You going to be okay looking after Sammy?"

"I'll be fine, my mother is here."

"Yeah, big help."

"Be nice."

"Call me if there is any problem?"

"Sure. Where are you going, Starbucks?"

"Yep," I say, unplugging the laptop.

"Heading out?" Barbara asks, looking up from the couch over the top of *Vogue*.

"Yeah, going to do a little writing down at the coffee shop."

"Oh, so you're still trying to do that, are you? What's it called, *The Ice Cube?*"

"*The Cube People.* I finished it two Christmases ago."

"Oh, well good for you, Colin. Any luck getting it published?"

"Not yet, but one publisher asked to see the whole thing."

"Well, that's encouraging isn't it? Who's Maggie Woodland published with? She's written science fiction."

"Cold Bird Press."

"Have you tried them?"

"No."

Barbara doesn't say anything, just leaves it hanging. Sarah walks up behind me carrying Sammy.

"I'll be back in a bit," I say. I kiss Sarah and a sleeping Sammy on the top of her little head. I go out the door.

Hungry Hole

Chapter 11

When Ryan opened the door, he saw Gillian's face, but it was much older, wrinkled. The hair was grey and she was wearing bifocals. "Hello Heidi," said Ryan, concealing the ball-peen hammer in his hand behind his right leg.

"I've been so worried, where's Gillian?"

"She's right upstairs. I don't know what happened. She came home early from work complaining she wasn't feeling well and then she wanted me to call you. She wanted to see you. She seems to have a low-grade fever. Maybe you can convince her to go to the hospital."

"Yes of course," said Ryan's mother-in-law as she stepped into the hallway and headed up the stairs.

When she'd reached the third step, Ryan swung the hammer, striking her in the back of head. Her arms shot out to the sides as if she'd been crucified. Ryan dodged her body as it fell backwards. When she landed, she twitched and convulsed. She shook all over, then became still. Her mouth and eyes were wide open. Ryan pulled her by the feet toward the basement. Her head bounced on the steps on the way down.

* * *

When Ryan came back upstairs, Gillian was standing in the hallway.

"Is that my mother's car out front?"

"Yes," said Ryan without any hesitation. "She stopped by to see us."

"Really? Where is she?"

"She's in the basement."

"The basement? What is she doing down there?"

"She brought us a surprise."

"What is it?"

"I can't tell. Then it wouldn't be a surprise now would it?"

Gillian moved down the dark hall without noticing the blood trail she was stepping on.

"Mom?" she called down the basement stairs.

"Go down, you should see it."

"Mom?" she called again. "Are you down there?"

"Go on."

Gillian took a few steps down, then stopped. "What's that smell?"

"You have to see it Gillian, with your own eyes. It's really quite something."

"Mom?" Gillian turned around to go back up the stairs but Ryan was right behind her. "I don't like this Ryan. Where's my mom?"

"Down there."

"Why isn't she answering then?"

"Maybe she can't hear you. You should..." Over Gillian's shoulder he saw the tentacle slither up the stairs. Gillian's eyes widened in terror as the tentacle wrapped around her leg, pulling her backwards. Gillian screamed. "Oh God, Ryan! Help me!" Gillian shouted as she was pulled to the bottom and around the corner.

My cellphone rings.

"Hello?"

"Hi, it's me," says Sarah. "My mother left for the hotel, so the coast is clear. I'm sorry she's such a pain."

"Yeah, me too."

"Can you come home? Sammy did a poop. I think we should try to give her a bath. She smells."

"Okay, I'll be home in ten. Want anything?"

"Espresso chocolate brownie if they have one. If they don't, don't worry, I don't want the low-fat vegan one. Otherwise get me something good. And a decaf with milk."

"Done. You know, my character just killed off his wife."

"You're a sick bastard. Does she get hacked up into little pieces?"

"I think you're the sick one... hacked up into little pieces?"

"Yeah baby, lots of blood. Hurry home will you?"

"Bye."

"Bye."

"I'm sorry Gillian," said Ryan. He stood on the stairs, listening to the slurping and squelching sounds the hole emitted as it devoured his wife.

What have I done, thought Ryan. What have I done?

The Darkness and the Light

Somehow I managed to endure four days of Barbara. In the evenings Sarah let me escape to Starbucks so I could work on *Hungry Hole*. I kept revising the part where Ryan hit his mother-in-law with the hammer, each time making it more bloody and violent. By the end of the fourth day, Ryan was mashing her head into a pulpy mess before sawing her up and feeding her to the hole, limb by bloody limb.

After the departure of Barbara, we came under siege by a barrage of visitors and non-stop phone calls from people wanting to wish us well, wondering when they could come and drop off a casserole, when they could come and see the baby: my mother, my father, Phil, Sarah's sister, my stepsister, my cousin and a number of Sarah's girlfriends. The apartment is swarming with flowers, cards, balloons and stuffed animals.

About a week later, I come home after getting groceries to find Sarah sitting on the couch holding Sammy. A helium foil balloon, slightly deflated, the word *Congratulations* written on it, floats mid-air, hovering just above and to the left of Sarah's head. Sarah's crying. My heart jumps. "What's wrong?"

"I don't know," she sobs.

I rush over. "Something wrong with Sammy?"

"No, she is f-fine," she cries.

I sit down beside her and rub her back.

"What is it baby? What happened? Why are you crying?"

"I don't know. I'm just sad. I'm okay, just sad."

"Sad about what?"

"I think it's just hormones, Colin. I'm still bleeding. I'm still being held together with string. I'm covered in breast milk. I haven't had a bath in two days. I haven't been outside in forever, and I'm so tired."

"Why don't I put away the groceries and then when I'm done, why don't I sit with Sammy while you take a bath? Then, if you're feeling up to it, we could go for a walk. I think the fresh air could do you some good. What do you think?"

She nods her head, tears streaming down her cheeks.

"Okay then, let me put those away and you get cleaned up."

I can't say that I'm too shocked by Sarah's emotional outburst. Just the other night we were watching *March of the Penguins* on TV. Sarah fell asleep. When they got to the part where one of the penguins loses his egg and the baby dies, I cried my eyes out. I can't imagine what's going on with Sarah and her superhighway of hormones surging uncontrollably around her body. While Sarah is in the bath, I place Sammy on the Baby Einstein activity gym. She is far too young for it, but it's supposed to be good for little Sammy's developing brain to look at black and white stripes. I log on to my email, which I haven't checked since I sent out the birth announcement. I have twenty new messages, most of which have the same subject line: "Re: Our

New Taxpayer," friends and family responding to the photos of Sammy I sent. One subject line grabs my eye: *The Cube People*. I click on it.

From: Marcus Jackson Editor Black Forest Editions
Date: 2007/04/25 AM 10:12:01 EDT
To: Colin MacDonald
Subject: The Cube People

Hello Colin:
After reading over your complete manuscript of *The Cube People*, I'm delighted to tell you that we would love to publish it if it is still available. It is one of the most unique and interesting books I've read in a long time. I thought the characters were well-developed and robust. The plot is extremely clever; however I did find some sections confusing and think they could use a reworking. Overall though, it's really a fabulous book. We would be looking at next spring as a release date. Please let me know if the manuscript is still available.

Looking forward to hearing from you.

Best Regards, Marcus

"Holy shit," I whisper to the air. My head is spinning. I re-read it several times. I look down at Sammy who is staring up at the black and white bar. "I did it Sammy," I tell her. I listen to the bathwater stop. Should I tell Sarah? Should I interrupt the bath? I'm about to burst. I'll wait. I tiptoe dance around Sammy on the mat pumping my arms into the air. Then I go back to the screen and read the email one more time. I just can't believe it. First Sammy, now this. I'm undeserving. I don't remember auditioning for this play, but here I am with the starring role.

Sarah sees me on the couch with a beer in my hand and a smile from ear to ear. Sammy's now in the vibrating chair. "Hi," she says.

"Hi," I say back, smiling like a lotto winner.

"What?"

"Black Forest Editions said yes."

"What? Really?"

I point to the laptop. "Read it."

Her hair wrapped in a towel, Sarah shuffles in her bathrobe over to the screen and reads. She stands up straight and turns around, right hand on her mouth. Her left hand is flapping, swatting away an imaginary bug as she begins to cry.

"I'm so happy, I'm sorry I'm crying, but I'm really happy for you, baby."

I go over and give her a hug.

"Are they a good press?"

"Well it's not a big press, but they have published a few Governor General's nominees."

"Oh baby, I'm so happy for you."

"You up for a walk?"

"I'm worried about popping a stitch."

"We'll go slow. I'll push the stroller. Maybe walk to the 7-Eleven and get a Slurpee?"

She nods her head.

"Look at little Sammy, isn't she beautiful?" I ask.

"She's so lovely. I love her so much."

"Man, can it get any better than this?"

I go back to work after being off for two and a half weeks. I have almost two hundred emails to wade through. There are several emails from management stating that they are toying with the idea of having a no-email day. I wish. I hack away at the electronic jungle of messages most of the morning. I'm happy to see that Jackie and Mr. Peaches are still gone. I'm secretly hoping that they'll be unable to come back. To my surprise, Dan shows up at quarter to eleven carrying a massive white panel. "Colin, give me a hand with this," Dan huffs.

"Jesus, I thought you were gone for good? Bruce told me you had fibromyalgia and you weren't coming back."

"Nah, turns out I have Seasonal Affective Disorder and I just need light."

"But, Dan, it's May."

"Well it's more like non-seasonal depression."

"Non-seasonal depression, what the hell is that?"

"Well it's seasonal depression, except it's not in the winter or fall."

"So you're suffering from just plain old depression then?"

"Well, sort of, I guess," says Dan cheerily. "The doctor told me I could use some light after I told him how dark my cubicle was." I suspect that this whole business is just a clever ruse for Dan to get what he really wants and has been asking for for years, namely a window seat.

We spend the next half hour attaching the metal stand and adjusting the height of the giant light panel. When Dan flicks it on, the whole quad is immediately awash in a powerful fluorescent light. It's football stadium light, the kind you would see on your way to heaven. I realize that I won't be able to work when Dan has his SunSquare Plus ablaze. It feels like a car is parked behind me with its high beams on. "Dan, I can't see my screen with the glare coming off of it, you're going to need to turn that thing off."

"Just fifteen minutes twice a day," pleads Dan. "I really need to get better."

"Christ, fine. I'll be back in fifteen then," I tell him.

I march off to get a coffee.

The Bottom of the Hole

Being back in the office, it seems like I've joined a secret club that only fathers can understand. You don't really know what it means to have a child, the sleep deprivation, the emotional influx, until you go through it yourself. I pass by Bob Roland on my way to the coffee room. Bob has three kids. "How's it going, Colin?"

"Pretty good. Tired."

"Don't worry, you'll never sleep again," he laughs. "But seriously though, don't worry, it will get better in three months or so. Oh, and you'll never sleep again."

He walks off laughing. "Thanks Bob, thanks for that."

I walk into the coffee room and there's Barry, Bruce and Dexter. They all turn their heads and look at me. I think they're going to say congratulations, or be jovial or something, but instead Barry says "Colin, we need to see you this afternoon in my office."

"Um, sure, what's it all about?"

"We'll discuss it then."

"Okay, what time?"

"1:30."

"Okay, see you then."

Dexter Peterson is in his fifties. He's a Tech-4 or Tech-5, I'm not sure which, but he knows everything. He's the guru's guru, the man behind the curtain, the mainframe god. Dexter stories are legendary around the office. He has appeared in people's cubicles and told them that their programs are using too much CPU, then rips their code apart leaving them decimated. You never want to see Dexter.

This little encounter leaves me shaken. I wonder if Dexter is part of the "we" in "we need to see you?" Maybe it's just Barry using "we" to mean "I?" It's probably just about my family leave or something. Still, I wonder if one of my programs I took over from Dan is sucking up too much CPU? I know there's some spaghetti code that I still need to fix. Perhaps I'm too paranoid?

Powering through the thousands of emails that have accumulated, I arrive at one with the subject line "No-Email Day." Clicking it open, a message from the Commissioner greets me.

To All MRC employees:

In today's rapidly growing technology age, information is coming at us at an almost incomprehensible rate. We have less and less time to get on top of the data that we are being bombarded with on a daily basis. Hours of each and every day are wasted sifting through email while the real work continues to accumulate. The excellent level of service to the national taxpayer is being hindered by email. It has to stop. We are going to be implementing a No-Email day so you have time to get to the real work. We live in challenging times, but working together we can be a glowing example for others of what a forward-thinking Agency we continue to be.

– Bill Crow, Commissioner of the Ministry of Revenue Collection

---

I smell disaster. I delete the email and move on.

I have lunch with Phil at Sunshine Valley. He and Zoe apparently had a big fight last night and we have to sneak by First Choice. I tell Phil the news about my book and he becomes more animated than he normally is. I can't believe how excited he gets. I love his reaction.

On the high about the book (Phil's contagious enthusiasm pushing it to the heights of Everest) combined with the secret-club-of-dads sensation I'm carrying, I feel electric. With this emotion radiating from my being, I waltz into Barry's office at 1:30 on the dot. Barry, Bruce, Dexter and two men in dark jackets who could quite possibly be from the cast of *The Matrix* are standing there looking like they have all eaten one too many serious pills.

"Whoa, what's up?"

"Please take a seat and shut the door," says Barry. I do. "This is Detective Bellows and this is Detective Waters from the RCMP," offers Barry.

I nod. Everyone is quiet, solemn. "What's up?" I ask.

Waters begins. "We're investigating Peter Cann for fraud. Do you know anything about it?"

"Fraud? No," I say.

"Do you recognize these?" asks Dexter, shoving a piece of paper at me. I take it.

"These are our test SINs."

"Test SINs?" inquires Bellows.

"Yeah, we use these social insurance numbers to test our system in production, in our live system. We use them all the time."

"Do you know what Peter was doing with them?" asks Waters.

"I don't know, testing the system?"

"He was filing them," says Dexter.

"What do you mean filing them?" I ask.

"With some of our calculations, we round down to the dollar. Peter was accumulating all the rounded cents that get dropped. This kind of fraud has been committed by many others in the computer programming field before; however none of them were this good. He put logic into place to hold the money in queues, which he would drain out every six months. It must have taken Peter at least ten years to put it into place, all the programs and logic in hundreds of programs needed to bypass all the checks," says Dexter with a hint of pride in his voice, as if only one of his own could be smart enough to pull it off.

"Wow, how much did he take?"

"We've been working with Dexter here to determine just that," says Waters. "We're estimating in the millions, maybe even upwards of a hundred million dollars, stolen from the government. If we catch him, and we will, he's going to be put away for a long time."

"Jesus, I can't imagine Peter doing something like that. It's crazy," I say. Now, that's what I say, but I'm thinking that Peter Cann is even more brilliant and more courageous than I imagined him to be. I'd been working beside a master criminal for years and never even knew it.

"The reason we wanted to see you Colin," says Dexter, "is your user ID is on some of the programs that we suspect Peter wrote."

"Really?" I stammer.

"Do you know how to code in Assembler?" asks Dexter.

"No, but I'm sure I could learn," I say.

Dexter looks at the two detectives and says, "I don't think he did it."

"Did what?" I ask. Jesus, I feel my face flush, my palms are sweating. Shit, I think about all my writing I have saved on the LAN. I think about the marker I took home to mark those boxes when we moved. I think of the extra fifteen minutes I took at lunch the other day. Jesus, has Peter set me up as some sort of fall guy?

"Help Peter," says Bellows.

"No way guys, I didn't do anything."

"Why is your user ID on a bunch of Assembler modules in Production?" asks Waters.

"Yeah, why?" pipes in Bruce. The joy that I had been radiating turns to irritation and I'm overcome with a desire to slap Bruce in the face, hard.

"I don't know. Maybe Peter did it under my user ID?"

"Colin, what we know is this. Peter has had his fingers in lots and lots of code. Pretty much everywhere he's put in bypass logic for these test SINs. Nobody's ever questioned what he was doing because they were just test SINs, and Peter is a well-respected and very smart man. None of the programs that we suspect he wrote have his user ID on them. He was good at covering his tracks. The other reason I don't think you did it is because Dan's user ID is on some of these programs. He could never write code this sophisticated, plus he wasn't physically at work when some of these programs were put into Production," says Dexter.

"So what do you want with me?"

"Well, we can't prove Peter did it *yet*. We also can't prove you didn't do it," says Waters.

"I didn't steal anything. I didn't code any Assembler programs. I don't have a clue what Peter did, but I'm telling you right now that I had nothing to do with it." I was nervous, not scared out of my mind, but nervous. I knew I'd done nothing wrong, but still, tell it to David Milgaard.

"Would you be willing to come down to RCMP Headquarters and make an official statement to that effect?" asks Bellows.

"Sure, sure thing," I say.

"Would you be willing to submit to a lie detector?" asks Waters.

"Yeah, for sure."

"Colin, until this mess is sorted out, you're going to have to leave work. I'm officially putting you on leave with pay until we find out more. We can't have you touching any code until you're cleared," says Barry.

"Mr. MacDonald, we're going to escort you out of the building. Would you be willing to come with us right now to Headquarters to make that statement?" asks Waters.

"Uh, what? Wait a minute. Did you say leave with pay?"

"Yes, that's right, you'll still get paid, but you aren't allowed to come into the office until you're cleared. If you've done nothing wrong, then there's nothing to worry about," says Barry.

"Okay, that's not so bad. Sure, let's go make that statement then," I say, standing up.

On my way out, Bruce in front of me, Waters and Bellows in tow, I notice that Suzy Scratch's desk has been cleaned out. "Where's Suzy Scratch?" I ask Bruce.

"Didn't you hear? She won it big. Two hundred and fifty

thousand. She left the next day."

"Son of a gun," I say.

I ride in the back of the cruiser. Waters and Bellows are quiet the whole ride there. The grey Kafkaesque building greets us with an impersonal politeness that I would only expect from a prison. We go inside, clear the security gate, and walk down a long hall to a windowless room with a camera mounted in the ceiling corner and a table and two chairs in the centre. On the table rest some paper and pens, a tape recorder, and some cords.

"Is that thing recording?" I ask, pointing to the camera.

"Yes, it is, Mr. MacDonald."

They clip a little microphone to my shirt. I flash to *Dateline* and all the false confessions that I've watched innocent people make during interrogations. Will they break me for something I didn't do? My heart is a jackrabbit being chased by a fox. Waters sits across from me. Bellows remains standing, arms crossed. I recognize it's their job to make people nervous, and because of this fact, I relax, just a little bit. They ask me all sorts of questions about myself, about my job, my education, Sarah, where we met, how long we've been together, etc. Then they grill me on Peter. Everything you could imagine. Did we ever go for lunch together? Did I ever see Peter outside of work? Did Peter have a dog or a cat? They ask me about Bruce, Dan, Brita and Carla. Finally Waters says, "Well I think that'll do for now." I look at my watch. I've been in here for almost three hours.

"Remember," says Bellows, "if you've lied about anything you've told us, you could be in serious trouble."

I sign an affidavit that what I've said is true. Then they drive me home.

Sarah's sitting on the couch when I walk through the door. She sees me and the tears erupt. "You okay?"

"I've got some bad news for you, Colin," she says.

"Is that why you're crying?"

"No, that's just hormones I think. I don't know, I just feel bad."

"Well I have a crazy story for you. I think mine will take a while to tell, so you tell me your bad news first."

"I think you're going to be upset."

"Lay it on me. It couldn't get much worse for me today."

"A woman, Nona I think her name was, called from Black Forest Editions."

My heart sank. "Oh God, don't tell me. They don't want to do it, Marcus changed his mind?"

"Not exactly. Marcus is in the hospital."

"What?"

"Marcus had been acting rather oddly and he was committed to the mental hospital."

"You have to be shitting me? Committed? What the fuck?"

"Sorry baby, Nona told me that all new publishing projects are being put on hold until they know what's happening with Marcus. She said it's a small press, that Marcus *is* Black Forest. She said she'll let us know."

"Is he going to be alright? Fuck. Fuck. Fuck."

"Sorry baby."

I see Sammy in her chair. Her face contorts, turns a light shade of red. She is taking a poop.

"Could you change her? I've done five today already."

I wipe Sammy's stinky butt clean. I get a beer from the fridge and slump down on the couch beside a weeping Sarah.

"I'm going to be home for a while," I say.

"What?"

"Christ, what a day," I say and take a swig.

Winter Rain Press
PO Box 1230
Toronto, ON
M5T 7H7

May 20, 2007

Dear Colin MacDonald:

Sorry for the lengthy time in responding; however, we are
working with a skeleton staff. We are unfortunately not able to
accept any new manuscripts at this time as we are booked up
for the foreseeable future.

Best of luck with your writing.

Sincerely,

James Johnston
Editor, Winter Rain Press

Insane

Sarah is taking the train to Toronto with Sammy for the weekend to visit her mother and her Aunt Molly. I was going to go, or at least protest strongly that I needed to go, that she couldn't take the baby by herself, but all I said was okay when she suggested I stay home. I'm hoping that this little trip will do her some good, snap her out of her funk. I wait with them at the train station until they board. I kiss Sarah and a sleeping Sammy goodbye. Sarah's on autopilot, as if she's sleepwalking. I remind her to call me day or night if she has any problems.

Now they're gone and I'm alone. Standing here in the vast emptiness of the train station makes *me* feel like crying. I immediately regret my decision not to go with them. I find my cell and call Phil. He says he'll be over later with beer. He sounds so fucking happy. Maybe I've made yet another bad decision?

Arriving home it feels as if I'm in somebody else's apartment. It's so quiet. I'm acting out somebody else's life – single with no kids.

I sit down on the couch and stare at my most recent rejection letter. It's lounging on the coffee table, waiting to give me a paper cut, the little bastard. Involuntarily my mind flashes to an image of Marcus Jackson. I picture him red-faced, hair wild and knotted, screaming in a straitjacket of a padded cell, the pages of *The Cube People* littering the floor around him. Maybe I can't write? I hunt down a copy of my manuscript from the closet to have a read. I haven't looked at it in over a year. When I hit page twenty, my guts feel like they're spilling out onto the floor. Suddenly it hits me: I can't write worth a fart. I'm horrific, and not in a good Stephen King kind of way either. No, the prose that lies here before me is awful. Has anyone actually read it and thought it was good? Just Peter Cann and Marcus Jackson: a thief and a mental patient. How long have I wanted to be a writer? I go to the closet and pull down my shoebox of rejection letters. I don't know why I keep them – maybe in the hope that one day I'll be able to say, "Ha! Look at all the fools who rejected my genius!" But sadly I'm realizing that maybe I'm not a genius, not even close. Suddenly I'm exhausted; my limbs are heavy. I go lie down. I fall asleep.

I open the door to Phil holding a two-four of Moosehead.

"Were you sleeping?" asks Phil.

"Yeah, I was lying down," I croak. "What time is it anyway?"

"Five. Shit man, you look like *Night of the Living Dad*, he blurts, barging his way past me. "Fatherhood got you that tired?"

"I don't think I can write," I tell him, following him toward the kitchen.

Phil opens the refrigerator door, pops the top of the beer case and unloads the beer into a crisper drawer. "What are you talking about, writer's block or something?"

"No, I'm talking about the fact that I suck donkey nuts. I can't write a fucking sentence."

"I don't understand. Here, have a beer," he says, unscrewing a cap and thrusting a bottle toward me.

"My publisher was committed to the nuthouse."

"Fuck off, really?"

Over the course of a couple of beers, I explain what happened to Marcus, and that what little optimism I had from publishing a couple short stories and a poem was now completely gone. Phil tells me this is total bullshit, that I can write the pants off of a mannequin on layaway. I don't understand what Phil says sometimes; I just go with it. He grabs my manuscript, thumbs through it, and reads aloud from a few pages in a Shakespearean actor voice. When Phil is reading, it doesn't sound half bad. Maybe it's not awful, just not very good.

Sarah calls to let me know that she got in safe and asks what I'm doing. I tell her and she playfully scolds me, warning me not to get too drunk. I ask how she's feeling. She says good and tells me she'll call me tomorrow. I'm not sure whether to believe her or not – about the feeling-good part that is. After more beer, Phil says we need to order pizza from "the best goddamn place in the entire city." So we do. Then he roots around in his backpack and wrenches out a mighty plastic bag of his so-called "boom weed."

"Listen man, I don't think I can smoke that. I haven't smoked pot in ages."

"Dude, this shit is crazy, you'll love it. Plus look what I brought over, the latest cut," says Phil, holding up a DVD of one of my favourite films, *Blade Runner*. Despite my protests about my inability to handle pot, Phil grabs his rolling papers and rolls himself a larger-than-cigarette-sized joint. "Listen man, you're not going to get a chance to light up for a long while, now that you're a responsible dad and shit. So, take full advantage of this weekend and party your ass off. Besides, tomorrow you can sleep the whole thing off."

I'm just finishing off my fourth beer. I feel great. A little pot. What's a little pot? Pizza, beer, a little pot, and *Blade Runner*: a winning combo. "Fine, but we have to smoke it out on the balcony."

"Let's roll," says Phil.

I inhale the first toke deeply, then proceed to expel smoke through a series of coughs and hacks for the next several minutes. I feel no effects. "I thought you said this was strong stuff," I wheeze.

"Just wait till it kicks in," says Phil, taking in a series of tiny sucks.

He passes it back and I take another hit, but this time I don't inhale as deeply. Again I repeatedly gag and choke as I exhale. As we approach the end of the joint, I hear the doorbell. It's the pizza guy. I leave Phil to finish it and run to get the door. As I open it up, I experience a strange sensation at the back of my neck and head, a warm heaviness crawling up the inside of my skull and wrapping itself around my brain. There before me stands a six-foot Rastafarian, a mass of dreadlock hair wrapped high above his head in what looks to be a beehive made from the Jamaican flag, boosting his height to almost seven feet. I realize at this moment that I'm stoned out of my tree. High as a tree, a tree with a kite stuck in it. High as a kite... is that where that comes from?

"'Ere be your Pizza pie man," sings the Rastafarian with a warm deep voice that reminds me for some strange reason of Ricardo Montalbán, even though he's Mexican. I stand in awe, feeling slightly dizzy, my heart picking up speed. His nostrils twitch ever so slightly as he sniffs the air. If I hadn't been stoned I probably wouldn't have caught the nostril flare.

"'Ey man, are you getting groovy with the night?" he asks me. He must realize I'm stoned, must be able to smell the pot – groovy with the night? I'm groovy with the night. I glance out the window and it's still not dark yet, not night. "Groovy, yes," falls out of my mouth, like a small child trying to throw a bowling ball, *kur-thump*.

"Excellent, mon. Dat will be twenty-two dollars, mon." Twenty-two dollars. The words echo around my head. Twenty-two dollars. Money. I reach into my pocket for money. My heart is doing jumping jacks.

"Rasta Jack!" yells Phil, appearing next to me.

"Philip, my mon, whatcha doing here?"

"Getting groovy with the night, my brother," says Phil. At this comment, Rasta Jack laughs. I can see all of Rasta Jack's teeth when he laughs. Little marshmallows. One of them is gold. Maybe he's a Jamaican pirate?

"This is my buddy Colin," says Phil, introducing me.

"Fantastic mon," says Rasta Jack, smiling and laughing. All I can do is nod my head. I'm shaky. My heart is doing a whole callisthenics routine. I need to remain calm. I need to go sit down.

"Colin, you gonna give him the money?" asks Phil. Money? All I can think about is how to express that I'm having a heart attack, but the words aren't coming out. Too much detail. I can't believe how fast the dope took effect. Money? Rasta Jack is looking at me strangely. I look to Phil for help.

"In your hand. Give Rasta Jack the money that's in your hand, dude." My hand extends involuntarily: somebody else's hand, an actor's hand.

"Tank you mon," says Rasta Jack, taking the money and passing Phil the pizza. "You need change?"

Change? I'm going to die standing up. How fast can a human heart go before it explodes? "Keep it," says Phil, coming to my rescue.

Phil invites Rasta Jack to smoke another, but Rasta Jack says he's got to deliver more pizza pies. I manage to stagger over to the couch and fall back into its exquisitely comfortable fabric. My heart's doing a heavy-metal drum solo. I'm trying to stay calm. I'm trying to focus on the juiciness of the couch.

"You want a slice now, or do you want to wait a bit?" Phil asks. I shake my head and he says he'll throw it into the oven on low to keep warm. My mind is racing. Thump thump thump thump thump thump thump thump my heart is going. Phil comes back into the living room. "It's wild shit eh?"

I nod.

"Want to watch *Blade Runner*?"

I nod. Phil puts the movie on and sits down beside me grinning from ear to ear. I wish I could express to Phil how much detail I'm processing at an incomprehensible rate. I'm a rollercoaster. I'm the Flash. I'm light.

As the movie plays, I try to calm myself down, try to relax. We watch Harrison Ford running around in a dark and rainy future. I think about artificial intelligence. I think about my character Setrac Sed from *The Cube People*, about how he too doesn't know that he's just an android. Maybe I'm just an android? Maybe I just got here and all of my memories are implants? Maybe I'm going to have to be committed to the hospital like Marcus Jackson? Maybe it was *The Cube People* that pushed him over the edge? Maybe my writing is so bad that it drives people insane? My heart had slowed, but now it's picking up speed again. I ride the next giant wave of panic. My thoughts are contorting, looping around on themselves. How can I think about my thinking? Can I not think about thinking? Where's the choice?

I grab my beer and swig. It doesn't seem very cold. I glance over at Phil who's wearing a perma-grin like the Joker. I can see every tiny pore on his face. He looks insane. My eyes move back to the TV and I get lost in the movie and in my own mind. As I watch Daryl Hannah do screaming back flips, I realize I'm absolutely famished. "I need to eat," I croak.

"Thought you would never ask, let alone talk again," says Phil, running to get the pizza. When I take a big bite of Rasta Jack's pizza pie, I'm sure there are angels weeping. If God could be found and eaten in the form of cheese, sauce and dough, then I've found God. He's in my mouth.

"I think my tongue just had an orgasm," says Phil, chewing a mouthful of pizza.

"The bacon, mushrooms, and onions are having group sex in my mouth."

"Fucking what I told you dude, best pizza in the goddamn city."

I devour four large slices of pizza as we watch the movie. Phil jumps up when it's over and is talking a mile a minute about what a fucking genius Ridley Scott is. He tells me we need to go to the 7-Eleven for gum and chocolate. When we arrive, the lights of the store are blinding and Angie the freaky cashier is working; her hair is now dyed a dark shade of pink. The whole thing is making my heart thump and bump in the most horrible way. I tell Phil that I need to wait outside.

It's 2 a.m. and I've finally come off my high. My mind feels like it has been birthed out of Amy Winehouse's vagina. Now I'm just drunk and tired. Phil thanks me for the night and says he's gotta split. He and his buddy are going rock climbing in the morning and he offers for me to join them. I say no, thanks, as I'm going to try to get some writing done. That's probably not true. I just don't want to go rock climbing.

I awaken but keep my eyelids closed, letting the fog of sleep evaporate slowly. I can smell Sarah on the bedding. Opening my eyes, I see the framed photograph of myself holding Sammy at the hospital on her first day of life. My father had one just the same, holding me. I remember the day my father left us: I went to my parents' bedroom and took that photo. My mother was downstairs in the kitchen crying. I snuck outside. She caught me trying to set it ablaze in the backyard. She smacked me across the face. With mascara running down her face she told me that my father was my father, that he was sick and needed help, and I needed to love him anyway. We never spoke of the incident again.

The phone rings. It's Sarah. "Are you still sleeping?"

"Ah, yeah, just getting up."

"Christ, it's almost noon. Sammy had a horrible night."

"Oh, I'm sorry."

"I miss you."

"I miss you, too."

"My mother's a witch," she whispers.

"What happened?"

"Same old shit. Tell you when I'm back. Listen, I'll call you later. Sammy's crying, I have to go. Pick me up tomorrow?"

"See you then."

"Bye."

"Bye." I hang up. A metallic taste lingers in my mouth, my

guts are full of air, and my head is throbbing. Thankful that I don't have to deal with a crying baby in my rotten brain state, I wander out into the living room in my underwear, rubbing my temples. The sun is pouring in through the window, illuminating the debauched contents of the coffee table: an empty pizza box, empty gum wrappers, beer bottles with the labels peeled off, the *Blade Runner* DVD case, a half-eaten bag of salt and vinegar chips, rolling papers, my shoebox full of rejection letters and my printout of *The Cube People*. It all sits there, a big heaping pile of stupidity and failure.

This is not somebody else's life. This is mine.

Goddamn Crackheads

It's nice being off, even if it's under the threat of possible imprisonment. But Sarah seems no better since returning from her trip. I'm wondering if this is just the baby blues, a small hormonal blip, or if we're moving into full-on postpartum depression? Sammy's playing on her mat. It's a beautiful spring day outside. I'm thinking some fresh air and a change of venue is just what Sarah could use. I could also use that. Maybe I can get some writing done in the park? I walk to our bedroom and see Sarah lying in bed, gently weeping. "Baby?"

"Yeah," she answers from the cocoon of blanket.

"Want to take a walk, or maybe drive down to Dow's Lake and have a picnic, get some fresh air?"

"I'm sorry Colin."

"Sorry about what?"

"Sorry about this. I don't know why I'm so sad."

"It's okay baby. How about a picnic?"

"Sure. Let me take a bath and get dressed."

"I'll pack us some sandwiches."

Sarah slides off the bed, still wrapped in the sheets and scoots over to me. I give her a hug. "Tell me it's going to get better," she says.

"It's going to be great, heck it's already great. We have each other, we're both young and healthy and we have a beautiful daughter."

"Isn't she cute?" says Sarah. And just as she says that, Sammy howls from the other room. We both dart in there and Sarah swoops her up off the mat. "I think she's hungry," Sarah says.

"Okay, you try to feed her and I'll make us lunch, then we can go after you've had a bath." I whip together a couple of beautiful sandwiches and make sure the diaper bag is well stocked. I put this stuff into the car along with a plastic tarp in anticipation of wet spring grass, a blanket, some trashy tabloid magazines for Sarah, Sammy's mat and my laptop. I need to finish off *Hungry Hole* while I'm on this paid leave. I assume it won't last for more than a week, but that might be enough time to have a first draft.

The breeze is cool coming off the water. Sammy has fallen asleep in her car-seat carrier. We eat our sandwiches in silence. Sarah seems better, calm. Tension drains away from me. "Do you mind if I write for a little bit?" I ask.

"Sure, pass me a magazine please."

Just then, Sammy wakes up and cries.

"I'll walk her around a bit, maybe she'll fall back asleep," I tell Sarah.

I push Sammy around for ten minutes but she's still screaming. I check her diaper. She's pooped through her outfit. I go back to the picnic area and Sarah helps me change the whole stinky mess. "Go on and do some writing," Sarah tells me as she latches Sammy on her breast.

I can tell Sarah is unhappy, that she'd rather go home, but she's trying to put on a good face for me. I flip open the screen on my machine, turn it on and type away. Fifteen minutes later I look up and Sarah is crying. "Why don't we go over and see Tom and Jen? They haven't seen Sammy yet. They'd love to meet her," I suggest.

"I don't know Colin, I don't think I'm up for it. Don't have the energy to put on a happy face."

Tom and Jen are my father's brother and his wife. They sent flowers with a card that said to call them when things have calmed down. They're good people. "Listen, I bet you one hundred bucks they'd invite us to stay for dinner."

"Jesus, dinner, I don't think I can."

"I just think you and me, especially you, have been cooped up too long. I think maybe some interaction with other people might be good. What do you say?"

"Okay," she says, but I sense she's agreeing just to please me.

Tom and Jen live over in Sandy Hill, in a two-storey brick home one block south of Rideau Street. It's a nice neighbour-hood near Ottawa University, bordering the downtown core. Unfortunately they live close to a bunch of crack houses. Tom and Jen tell us over dinner that they often find crack pipes and needles in their backyard.

"Such a shame," Jen says, shaking her head. "It was so lovely until those damn crackheads showed up. Now I'm afraid to walk alone at night. If Tom doesn't come with me, I don't go out." After all the gushing over Sammy, we eat a meal of lasa-gna, garlic bread and Caesar salad that Jen whipped up. Sarah puts on a great face to the point where I'm thinking that maybe she's actually feeling better. We eat homemade apple pie with ice cream and I'm so full that all I want to do is lie down. My uncle tries to push for a cigar on the back porch, but I tell him we ought to get going. I strap Sammy into the portable car seat and we are in the middle of saying goodbye when, SMASH! It's the loud sound of glass breaking. Uncle Tom opens the front door and steps out onto the small veranda. I follow him out.

When I took computer science, one of the things they drilled into my head early on was always, always, always make a backup. *The Cube People* is backed up at work and on disk. *Hungry Hole* on the other hand, well I haven't bothered to make a backup of this yet. I guess because it's not finished. I see a guy pulling my laptop from the front seat of our car through the opening where the windshield used to be. That laptop represents almost a year's worth of writing. The adrenalin and anger hit me and gets my lasagna-packed form moving past Tom and down the four steps of their home to the sidewalk. "Hey, stop!" I yell.

This longhaired kid, who I wouldn't say is more than twenty-five years old, sees me coming and takes off sprinting, laptop tucked under his arm. Holy shit, he's moving fast. Not today fucker, not today. I pour everything I have into it. His lead on me is still growing. He reaches the corner and hangs a right toward busy Rideau Street. I cut diagonally across the lawn, hopping a bush and make up some distance. He looks back and sees me still on him. I'm tired and my legs are burning. Son of a bitch. I push myself. There is no goddamn way I'm writing this novel again. Another block and he seems to be slowing. People on the street are watching us. Why doesn't somebody stop him? I'm too tired to yell out for him to stop, so I just keep running. Another block and I'm almost on him.

I reach out, arm stretched, and grab the back of his jacket and put on the brakes.

He releases my laptop and it goes spinning into the street. My eyes follow it as if it were the last-second shot of a tied basketball game. I let go of the kid and move to retrieve it but in that second, that oh-so-very-short second it takes to fly through the air and smash on the ground, it's already too late. I watch helplessly as a city bus roars by. My laptop rolls and tumbles under the wheels and I see it flip open. For another second it looks good, just sitting there waiting for somebody to turn it on and type away. But a second city bus follows, crushing the open jaw of my laptop flat. There are horrible crunching sounds. Plastic debris scatters the road. The *e* key lands by my feet like a tooth spit out by a boxer. I quickly dash out and grab what's left. The kid is long gone. I kneel on the sidewalk and try in vain to turn it on. Nothing. It's completely ruined.

"He went that way," offers a woman pointing down the street.

"That's okay, all the damage that could be done has been done."

"Goddamn crackheads," she says. "Somebody should do something about them."

My uncle has called the police. They show up and I give them a description of the guy. We spend forty-five minutes cleaning the glass out of the car. It's everywhere. On the drive home, I'm numb. "I'm so sorry, baby," says Sarah.

"No worries," I say. "I'll just rewrite it. Or maybe it was a sign, maybe it was awful. Maybe it was meant to be?"

Sarah doesn't say anything. We drive the rest of the way home in silence. After we get Sammy to sleep, I grab a beer from the fridge. I plunk myself down on the couch. I pick up our portable phone. It's beeping – messages. I punch in our code.

"Hello, this is Nona from Black Forest Editions. I have some rather bad news, I'm afraid. Marcus committed suicide last night. He was terribly depressed. The funeral will be in two days. Anyway, I wanted to let you know that all publishing projects are suspended indefinitely. I'm very sorry, but I suggest that you try to find another publisher for your manuscript. Best of luck to you, Colin. For what it's worth, I really liked *The Cube People*. Again, best of luck. Goodbye."

Sarah walks into the living room. "Anyone call?" she asks.

I get up and pour myself a stiff drink of whiskey and drink it down. Then I pour myself another.

"You don't have to drink just because you're mad," she says.

"The first was out of anger, the second is out of love." The booze burns in my mouth and gut and it feels real and right; the perfect complement to my anger. I probably shouldn't be drinking, but I won't be punching any holes in the walls, at least not today.

No-Email Day

I mope around the apartment the next day until Barry calls me and says that I've been cleared of any wrongdoing. Peter Cann was the mastermind behind the whole thing. I'm to return to work immediately. They're behind schedule and really need my help to get things back on track. I say great and hang up. Fuck.

I go into work the next day, walk to my cubicle and sit down at my desk. My chest tightens and my ears pulse. I find it hard to breathe. I spin in my chair. Somebody's cleaned out Jackie's desk; presumably it's her belongings sitting in the three big boxes which are atop her desk. Dan's therapeutic light box stands there reminding me of a hanging gallows. Carla's not in yet. I'm alone. I do my best to keep breathing, to stay calm. I grip the edge of the desk. My heart slows. I keep breathing. The air smells funny, like chemical cleaners. I'm okay, I'm going to be fine. I power on my machine and check my email: 212 new messages to plough through. Bruce appears in the doorway.

"Ah Colin, glad to see you're back. Listen, can you review these packages right away? They needed to be done last week," he says, dropping four or five thick file folders into my in-basket. "And remember, tomorrow is no-email day and bring-your-slippers-to-work day. You might not have heard about bring-your-slippers-to-work day. It's something Barry came up with to lighten the mood around the office, you know, make everyone feel like they're at home."

"Bring my slippers to work," I repeat mindlessly.

"Good stuff Colin," says Bruce.

I manage to get one program change completed before Phil shows up. His hair is orange. "What the hell dude?" I ask him.

"Zoe did it, you dig?"

"I thought you broke up?"

"We're getting married," he says smiling. "You inspired me, Mr. Domestic."

"Jesus."

"You look fucking awful dude, what's wrong with you? Sammy keeping you up?"

"Let's go and eat. I'll tell you all about it. Your head looks like a pumpkin."

"Johnny Rotten, baby."

"Jesus."

After lunch, I work away, a zombie. I'm detached. I'm going through the motions. I'm the substitute, the real worker will be here soon to replace me. I keep moving, keep at it. Sarah calls in the afternoon. She says Sammy misses me and I should hurry on home. "How are you feeling?" I ask her.

"I'm okay, just a little sad. How are you feeling?"

"I'm good," I tell her, lying.

"You sure?"

"Yeah, just a little tired is all."

"What do you want for dinner?"

"How about I pick something up?" I suggest.

"Just not pizza."

"Right, see you guys soon."

"Love you."

"You too baby," I say, hanging up. Then I pick up the phone and call her right back.

"Did the mail come?"

"Yes."

"Anything for me?"

"I didn't want to tell you. I opened it. Rejection letter from Big Shot Books."

"Okay, that's all I wanted to know."

"Sorry baby."

"Nah, it's fine. Give Sammy a kiss for me."

Sammy was up all night screaming. She had a fever – I ended up on the phone yakking to a Telehealth nurse at three in the morning to reassure Sarah that Sammy wasn't going to die. I barely got two hours of sleep. I'm a mess getting into work this morning. I brew myself a strong cup of coffee. The little red light on my phone is silently blinking: a message from a weary graveyard-shift person telling me one of my batch jobs abended in the night. I log onto my machine and automatically click on the Outlook icon. Up pops a message window stating that this application is unavailable at this time. Great, no-email day. I saunter over to Bruce's cubicle. He's wearing goofy bunny slippers that are impossible not to notice. "Nice slippers," I say.

"Colin, where are yours?"

"Forgot," I lie.

"I thought you might, so I brought you my extra pair," he

says, reaching into a bag that is sitting on the floor. Out comes a pair of fluorescent green slippers that I'm sure belong to Bruce's transvestite alter ego.

"Jesus," I say.

"Try 'em on."

"Not on your life."

"Please Colin, I've got Barry breathing down my back about this – team spirit."

"Forget it."

"Please Colin," he bubbles, as if this idiotic act of dressing up in casual indoor footwear will somehow place him in Barry's good graces.

"Fine," I say, taking the slippers. I put them on and to my surprise they're actually quite comfortable. "Listen, we have an abend."

"Do what you normally do Colin."

"Normally I'd email people about the problem."

"Not today," says Bruce, smiling cheerfully.

Back at my desk I log onto the mainframe and look into the problem. I trace through the computer dump and find out that we're being passed bad data from another group. We have a corruption issue on our hands and the consequences could be serious, possibly affecting thousands of tax returns. I habitually click on the email icon again and get the same "application is unavailable" message. Phones are ringing across the floor. I overhear Cindy from the Refrigerator Committee, who sits four cubicles over, yell, "Goddamn fucking email fucker." Cindy is a lovely lady, kind, considerate. This is what no-email day has done to her in only a few hours: it has given her Tourette's.

I quickly realize I'm going to have to wander around the floor and talk to people. I print off pieces of code and data so

I can show it to the people who are possibly impacted by the problem; normally I would just forward this in a floor-wide email. As I approach the printer to collect my sheets, I see the blinking red light of the machine that indicates it's out of paper. Usually there are extra refill bundles lying around, but today there are none. I wander down the hall. Standing before the secretarial throne, I watch Line scrutinize pictures of a house on a real-estate website. I wait for Her Majesty to grace me with an acknowledgement of my presence. Finally she glances up and asks me, as if I've interrupted some sort of Royal Tea, what it is that I want? "Paper for the printer. We're out," I drone.

"There should be some on the floor under the printer."

"None, all gone."

"Then there's no more paper."

"What?"

"Listen Colin, I'll make this easy for you. Barry was reluctant to sign the requisition form for more paper because of the whole Paperless Office thing. He eventually did sign, but we missed our delivery window by a day. So there's not going to be any more paper for the next two weeks."

"Any suggestions?" I ask.

"You can take five dollars from petty cash to buy paper at Office Land." I laugh. I continue to laugh. I laugh until tears are rolling down my cheeks. Line is looking at me like she's ready to call the nuthouse and I tell you I'm ready to go. I manage to calm down enough to say sure, give me the money. I don't know why, maybe it was the fumes coming off of Line, but I bum a smoke off a guy at the front door of my building. I smoke it on my way over to Sunshine Valley. It's disgusting, but I smoke it anyway. It makes me feel human. As usual, the mall is full of turtle-speed elderly shoppers that I duck and hop as I zigzag wildly down the corridor making my way to Office Land.

Quickly I find the cheapest paper, then go about assessing which of the two lines at the cash is the most expedient. In one line, I spy the old woman who I always see with her pink bathrobe and motorized scooter. She's wearing the exact same green slippers which, up until this moment, I forgot I was wearing. No one seems to notice or care. Old ladies always seems to be rooting around in the bottom of their black purses, trying to find the exact change for whatever it is they're buying. They always end up defeated and forking over a twenty-dollar bill. I pick the other line. Five minutes later, the woman in front of me is paying for a bag of office goodies with her credit card. The clerk slices the plastic card at the top of the handheld debit machine like she was cutting its throat. She stares at the device for a few seconds and swipes the card again. The look that registers on her face is, *It's not working.* She pushes some buttons on her cash and tries the card yet again. Nothing. The clerk calls over her manager and he inspects the machine. He tries to swipe the card. They try to reboot the machine to no avail. The manager apologizes and directs the woman in front of me to a neighbouring cash. The clerk looks at me and says, "Sorry sir, but I can only take cash." I wave the blue head of Sir Wilfrid Laurier triumphantly in the air and announce proudly, "Not a problem."

Back in the office, I load the paper cartridge drawer. The red light turns green and the printer hums, thankful for its feeding. It spews out all the documents that have been stored up in its memory queue. I grab a piece, hoping that my sheets are the first to be spit out. Looking at the page, the ink is barely visible. Fucking toner cartridge. I pop open the printer and it beeps angrily at me for interrupting. I pull out the black cylinder and give it a shake, the magic trick to squeezing a bit more ink out. As I'm doing this, Steve from the Refrigerator

Committee swishes by in blue and gold sequined slippers that look as if they were stolen from Liberace's wardrobe and says, "Did that yesterday, Colin. It's completely out of juice, honey bun."

I walk down to Line. "I need a toner cartridge for the printer."

"Nice slippers. The toner is on order."

"Can I have some more money from petty cash?"

"You just used the last five dollars."

I'm not laughing; I'm stunned. I stand there and listen to myself breathe. After a moment Line says, "Listen, Colin, this is a big building you know. There are other printers on other floors that use the same ink cartridge."

"Are you suggesting that I go and steal a printer cartridge from another floor?"

"I'm just saying that there are other printers in the building. That's all I'm saying," she says with a sly grin.

"I see. Thanks," I say and walk back to the printer, grab the toner cartridge and head to the elevator to go one floor up.

The floor above has exactly the same layout as my own. I march toward the printer. Often I see people I don't recognize wandering around my floor. I just assume they're there for a meeting or they're new staff; I never think ah ha, that's one of those bloody toner-cartridge thieves. I glance around nervously. A woman I don't know but recognize is walking toward me. "Hey, Colin, what are you doing up here? You going to the big Java meeting?" she asks me. How does she know my name?

"Yeah," I lie.

"Well come with me. I'm going there now. It's over here," she says spinning me around, away from the printer. Shit, how am I going to get out of this? I try to read her name off of her ID card, but I'm afraid she'll think I'm staring at her breasts.

"Do you always wear slippers at the office? And what's with that toner cartridge?"

"No, special day on my floor. Oh shoot," I say snapping my fingers. "I forgot my notebook."

"I can lend you some paper…"

"No, no, that's okay. I'll just meet you in there." I scurry back toward the printer. Nobody's around. I quickly do the switch and head back downstairs. When the printer resumes printing with its stolen internal organ, the pages again come out faded. I stole a dud. I spend the rest of the day walking around the floor, explaining the same problem over and over while we marvel at each other's cozy footwear.

Laura from the Refrigerator Committee came by today like some sort of Harlem pimp pushing her daughter's bland Girl Guide cookies. She's been doing this annually for many years now. How long can her daughter be in Girl Guides? I buy a box just to be polite. I move through the days on autopilot. I'm forever in an out-of-body experience. Sarah is sad all the time and Sammy only sleeps four hours at a time – sometimes five if we're lucky.

I find the first two chapters of *Hungry Hole* saved on my hard drive at work. I try to write it again, but can't do it. My life energy has been sucked dry. Sarah's on my case because I drink a bottle of wine with dinner every night. I'm drinking about six cups of coffee during the day. My panic attacks are becoming more intense. I now run to the handicapped washroom when I sense one coming on.

My cell rings. It's Sarah wondering where I've been, she's been trying to reach me at my desk. I note the time. I've been in the washroom for ten minutes staring blankly at myself in the mirror. I tell her I'm in a meeting and I'll call her back later. I go back to my desk. There's an email from detective Waters of the RCMP. I click on it.

Hungry Hole

Chapter 14

It was an eating machine and it owned him. Ryan had become
its slave, become its hunger. The hunger coursed through his
veins. It burned in his arms and legs like lactic acid. The hole
was hungry again. This morning's Girl Guide and her twelve
boxes of cookies hadn't satisfied it. It was afternoon snack time.

As Ryan lurched down the hallway like a drug addict in
search of a fix, he knocked a picture of his grandfather off the
wall. Hanging it back on the nail, he stared at his grandfather's
enormous handlebar moustache and remembered the shrivelled
old man he had become before he died in Saint Anthony's
Long-term Care Facility. Ryan thought of the drooling, wheel-
chair-bound seniors at the home. They were helpless; most were
incapable of comprehensible speech. They would make perfect
food.

Ryan purchased a light green nursing uniform from a medical
supply store before renting a cube van. He parked the van at
the shipping-receiving door at Saint Anthony's. He pulled out the
ramp and unlocked the van's back door. To his surprise the back
door of the building was locked. He rattled the door angrily.
"Nineteen eighty-four," said a female voice from behind him.

Ryan spun around to observe an attractive woman in white
nursing attire. "Pardon?" asked Ryan.

"Nineteen eighty-four. It's the code for the keypad lock,"
she smiled. "We don't want to let the patients wander out accidently."

"Heavens no," Ryan said. "They could hurt themselves hor-
ribly. Thanks."

"Don't mention it," she said, walking on and lighting a cigarette.

Once inside, Ryan found himself at an all-you-can-eat buffet.
Catatonic and lifeless elders littered the halls. One after the
other, Ryan rolled them out the back door and into the van.
Once in the van, he secured the victims to their wheelchairs
with plastic ties to make sure they couldn't pound on the side of
the van for help, even though he doubted they had that much
energy.

He had room for one more. In a sunroom with a few plaid
couches and many large potted plants, he found a lady in a
pink bathrobe and green slippers with oxygen tubes up her
nose looking out a large picture window. Her nametag read
Mrs. Barry. "Mrs. Barry, time to get you home for dessert," said
Ryan as he pushed her out the door.

* * *

The man at the medical supply store gave Ryan two thousand
dollars in cash for all the wheelchairs. "You get any more, come
to me first. I'll take them off your hands."

"I might have another load for you this afternoon," said
Ryan. "A lot of old people just falling off these days."

Six months later...

Crawling Out of the Hole

Sammy can now sit up and is sleeping six to seven hours straight a night. It's truly remarkable how a few extra hours of sleep can change your life. And Sarah is back to normal. She was depressed for about a month and half. It was Dr. Jekyll and Mr. Hyde, just a snap of the fingers and she was back. She woke up one morning and told me that she was feeling much better. She described it as being in a fog. She knew she wasn't herself, but there was nothing she could do about it.

Detective Waters had wanted more information on Peter Cann, who'd pulled a Houdini, disappearing off the face of the earth with millions of taxpayer dollars in his pocket. We ended up having several long discussions about Peter, and actually formed a friendship. When I told him about what had happened to my laptop, he asked me what I'd done with it. I told him nothing, that I'd bought a new one with the insurance money. "But did you throw it out?" he'd asked me.

"No, for some reason I've kept its plastic corpse in my closet."

"Bring it in. I'll have one of our data-recovery people take a look at it." That was two months ago. Well two weeks after I gave him the machine, he called and said that his people had recovered the complete contents of the hard drive. I had my *Hungry Hole* novel. Light came back into my life. The tightness of my cubicle walls receded, just a little.

I'm making dinner, stir-frying chicken and veggies in a wok. The phone rings. "Can you grab it? I'm changing Sammy," yells Sarah.

"Hello?" I say.

"Hello, is Colin MacDonald there please?" asks a voice that sounds vaguely familiar.

"Speaking."

"This is Nona Jenson calling from Black Forest Editions."

"Yes?" I'm excited. Nervous. My heart picks up speed.

"Kurt Jackson, Marcus's brother, was an editor over at Cold Bird Press. Well, he quit and has taken over Black Forest. He read *The Cube People* himself and loved it. If it's still available, we'd like to draw up a new contract and move ahead as soon as possible."

"Waaaahhhhhoooooo!!" I scream. I jump around, pumping my fists into the air. Sarah comes running into the kitchen carrying Sammy.

"What is it?"

"Black Forest... Marcus had a brother... He took over... They're still going to publish it!"

Sarah's face breaks into a huge smile and she dances in a circle with Sammy.

"Hello?" says Nona's voice

"Sorry," I say back into the phone. "I'm so excited. Okay, yes, it's all yours. Send me the contract. I'm ready to sign."

One year later...

A Cube at My Door

At my front door sits a box with the words *Black Forest Editions* printed across the top. I carry it inside and place it on the coffee table. It's heavy. I run to the kitchen and get a steak knife. I carefully cut the tape on the box and flip open the cardboard flaps. There before my eyes, neatly packed with crumpled paper along the borders of the box, are two stacks of *The Cube People*.

I reach in and delicately pull one out. I stare at the cover. There's my name printed in black letters, *Colin MacDonald*. Surreal. I turn it over in my hands and read the back cover. I flip it back around. Kurt Jackson must have worked his magic over at Cold Bird, because what I love best of all is the quote that sits near the top, adorning the cover: "A tour de force." –Maggie Woodland. I can't wait to shove that under Barbara's nose. I crack it open and read the inside cover. I read the dedication page: *For Sarah*. I flip the pages and smell their wonderful aroma of new paper.

The front door opens and Sarah walks through carrying Sammy in her arms. Sarah bends down and puts her on the ground. Sammy sees me and comes running over yelling, "Daddyyyyyy." I swoop her up in my arms and kiss her on the cheek.

"How's my Sammy Whammy?" I ask her.

"What dat?" she asks, pointing to my book I'm still holding in my hand.

"That's Daddy's book."

"Oh my God, it's here?!" yells Sarah.

She runs over and grabs the book from my hand. She looks at it, flips it over and flips it back.

"Oh my God, Maggie Woodland, a tour de force, you've got to be kidding me. Are you happy with it?"

"Over the moon."

"Juice, Daddy," orders Sammy.

"Okay little one, let's get you some juice," I tell her. Sarah follows us into the kitchen, reading the book along the way.

"I'm really proud of you, Colin."

"Daddy, juice," Sammy repeats impatiently.

"Okay, pumpkin, hang on, Daddy's getting it," I say, putting her gently down on the floor so she can play with the fridge magnets. I move her over slightly so I can open the fridge door and grab the apple juice.

"I'm really proud of you," repeats Sarah.

"Thanks baby," I tell her, popping the can. "I couldn't have done it without you."

The bus sways along and my eyelids are heavy. Sammy had a bad night. I ended up sleeping on the couch. Across the aisle sits a man. I recognize him from somewhere. It dawns on me: this is the man with the briefcase and the piece of Tupperware, microwavable leftovers inside, whom I had envisioned hanging himself. He looks exactly the same as when I last saw him over a year ago. I presume I look the same too, but I'm not. The bus slows to a stop and a few kids get on. I look out the window and stare at a crack in the pavement. Then I watch it disappear.

Four months later...

Marketing

From the table near me, the same three faces of a former prime minister stare at me as does the bikini-clad blonde from the *Sports Illustrated* swimsuit calendar from the rack close by. I'm sitting at a small beige table near the front of the Stanzas Bookstore in Sunshine Valley Mall. On my left is a wall of mass-market paperbacks by such authors as Stephen King, Ian Rankin, Maeve Binchy and Marian Keyes. On my right is a table with a giant black and white photo of Stanzas CEO Sophie Wiseman with a cup of coffee and a smile with an ever-so-slight seductive air, the promise of possible intercourse in front of the fire at the ski chalet. The words "Sophie's Choice" grace the top of the photo and her orange and purple stickers adorn the covers of Canadian books such as Brian Mulroney's autobiography. However the most coveted sticker, the one which is a licence to print money, is the sacred and revered oval of Oprah's Book Club. They will all go on to be *New York Times* bestsellers, if they aren't already.

On the table before me are twenty copies of my book and

a little cardboard sign shipped from my publisher that reads, *Colin MacDonald signs his exciting debut novel The Cube People from 10 am to 2 pm @ Sunshine Valley Mall.* I took the day off work so I could do this and hopefully sell a few books to colleagues cruising the mall on their lunch breaks. I sip my coffee and twirl the pen engraved with the words, *With Love Always, Sarah* – a present she gave me at my book launch. The store manager appears at my side. "Everything okay? You all set up here?"

I smile back, trying to be upbeat, but I realize after sitting here for the last twenty minutes without being able to engage a single store patron in conversation that I'm no J.K. Rowling. No one is lined up in costume to buy my book. "Yep, everything seems good to me," I tell her.

"Good. Just let me know if you need anything. I'll make an announcement over the PA system that you're here."

"Great, I appreciate it," I say, watching her slowly amble away. I spin my pen and stare at the *Sports Illustrated* calendar. Sarah and I are back on the fertility bandwagon. We're trying for a second child. The humpathon schedule is about to resume. I'm dreading it. I think that this *Sports Illustrated* cover may provide some fodder for a particularly rough evening when Sammy won't settle and we HAVE TO DO IT. I tuck the image into the back of my mind.

An elderly woman approaches with a warm smile and asks me which way the washroom is. I tell her. A few minutes later a man asks me if we sell greeting cards. I tell him that I don't know as I don't work here. He seems quite annoyed by my response and asks what I'm doing here if I'm not working but storms off in a huff before I can answer him.

A glance at my cellphone indicates that I've been sitting here for thirty minutes without even a single bite. I'm discouraged.

This has been my dream for years. Here I am, sitting in the country's biggest retail chain bookstore, and I'm having about as much impact as a light beer has on a hardcore alcoholic. Suddenly there's a crackle as the store's PA system kicks in. "Good morning shoppers," echoes the voice of the store's manager. "Today if you buy any three books you get the fourth free. Also today we have with us author Chris MacDonald signing his science fiction novel *The Cube Particles*. Please stop by and see Chris to get your copy today."

I'm fuming mad. Chris MacDonald? *The Cube Particles*? What the fuck? But just as quickly as I become mad, I realize that it makes no difference what my name is or what the title of my book is – I'm quite simply a nobody. Not a soul comes running over (or even slowly saunters for that matter). No one seems to take any notice that there was any announcement at all. A young attractive woman with a backpack wanders into my line of vision and I catch her gaze. "Hi, looking for some exciting reading?" I ask, trying to lure her in. However, as she comes closer, I realize she's quite young and probably still in high school – this makes me feel lecherous, spider-like. She picks up a copy of my book and flips it over in her hand and reads the back. I find myself suddenly nervous, as if I'm being graded, judged.

"This your first book?" she asks.

"Yes, first one," I say, still smiling away, feeling artificial, silly.

"Wow, cool. I want to write."

"Yeah? Cool."

"Did it take you long to write?"

"A couple of years, but it took much longer to get it published."

"I bet," she says, bobbling the book in her hands before placing it back on the table. "Sorry, but I'm a student, can't really afford it. I'm just in here to buy a textbook. Good luck though."

"Thanks, no worries."

I'm oddly both pleased and deflated. I drain back my coffee and wish I had a cigarette, not that I would be allowed to smoke it in here anyway. Maybe if I were Hunter S. Thompson? I bet they'd let J.K. Rowling smoke in here. Shit, they'd let her smoke whatever she damn well wanted. I bet they'd be bringing her giant wizard pipes packed to the brim with muggle marijuana if she were signing her book here. Over the next half an hour, a series of middle-aged women come by and tell me that although they think it's wonderful that I managed to get published, they don't read science fiction.

A tall, skinny man with long, thin hair, a ratty army jacket and thick body odour stops to tell me that he's working on a novel. I make the mistake of asking him what it's about. He blathers on for twenty minutes about a convoluted spy thriller that involves fifteen main characters and endless subplots. He finally leaves, telling me that he doesn't want to give too much away, in case I try to steal his material.

A stocky man, balding, his shirt open down to mid-chest, exposing a gold chain with a crucified Jesus resting in a thick mat of black chest hair, approaches my table. He gives me the impression of a bouncer or mechanic, a guy who works out at the gym, who's terribly strong, but drinks far too much beer and is constantly battling his gut. Someone who watches American football on Sunday with a plate of chicken wings after washing his sports car. Someone who's terribly illiterate.

"Hey," he says. "You write this book?"

Duh. Hello there, Mr. Dumbass? "Yep, I sure did."

He picks it up and inspects it. "You a local guy?"

"Born and raised here. I'm local produce," I tell him, smiling.

"Yeah, I've read a lot of Philip K. Dick, and Vonnegut, and I read *Dune* and some of Arthur C. Clarke's stuff, but I'm more into Elmore Leonard and Carl Hiaasen, you know, crime stuff like that. But Jon Krakauer, admire his stuff too."

I'm speechless. I marvel at how profoundly wrong I can still be about the people around me. In all the years that I've been walking around this earth of ours, I still, it seems, don't have a clue.

"Well if you enjoy Philip K. Dick, I'm sure you'll enjoy this."

"I'm sure I will," he says, smiling. "Will you sign it for me?"

"Um, sure, of course," I say, taking the book from him. "Who's this going to?"

"Make it out to Don."

For Don:
May this first impression be a good one.
Many thanks, Colin MacDonald

After he leaves, I see him in line at the cash with my book in his hand. I just sold my first book to someone I didn't know, someone who wasn't at my book launch. I couldn't be happier.

Don's sale triggers a flurry. My confidence grows with each patron who walks by my table. A few of my colleagues from work swing by as they said they would and buy a few copies. Phil turns up at noon bringing me a shawarma for lunch and buys another copy for his mom (he bought three at my book launch). He asks me if I'm ready for the weekend. He's getting married to Zoe in Montreal, where most of her family live. I'm the best man. It dawns on me that I still need to write a speech. Sarah calls on my cell to check on how things are going and reminds me that tonight we begin our fertility cycle. As I hang up, I see Barry's pudgy little form skipping toward me. His

Donald Duck tie and government ID tag are swishing back and forth in windshield-wiper style across his tummy.

"So here you are Colin. Almost forgot about your little shindig until I ran into Jack from the floor with a copy of your book. So, how goes sales? You going to be quitting any time soon?" asks Barry, laughing. Barry has a way of crawling under my skin like nobody else I know.

"I don't think any time soon."

"Well, Shakespeare," he says. The hairs on my neck stand on end. "Next week, I've got someone new joining your team. His name is Wolfgang and he'll be replacing Jackie. I need him to keep the handicapped washroom quota filled, so to speak."

"Is he also blind?" I ask.

"He has ADD," Barry responds cheerfully.

"What?" comes flying out of my mouth. For a split second I think Barry is pulling my leg, but then I realize this is Barry. He's not capable of such subtle and dark humour.

"Attention deficit disorder," explains Barry. "Wolfgang has a very hard time focusing on a task for more than a few moments. He loses his train of thought. ADD is a very serious disorder. I was hoping you would mentor him."

"Why in God's name does someone with ADD need a handicapped washroom?"

"He doesn't… but he's disabled according to the guidelines set out by the Ministry, and we can't really discriminate amongst the disabled now, can we?"

"I guess not," I say, hoping my body language isn't somehow betraying me.

"Okay, okay," says Barry, picking up a book. "I guess I better take one of these, Mr. Steinbeck. Throw your X in it," he orders, tossing the book to me.

To Barry:
The greatest manager that MRC has ever known.
Warm regards, Ernest Hemingway

He waddles to the cash, chuckling at my inscription.

The Wedding

On the suggestion of Zoe's parents, we booked a little B&B in Old Montreal down by the port close to the church where the ceremony will be held. It's a three-storey climb in an extremely narrow stairwell to our room and I lug an unwieldy stroller, a portable crib, my suit and two suitcases – though we're only staying one night. I make four trips and by the last one, I'm sweating up a storm. I tell Sarah I need to have a shower. The room has its own bathroom, but it's the smallest bathroom I've ever seen. After I get out, Sarah gets in (only room for one at a time) and sets off on an elaborate makeup ritual that she reserves just for special occasions. I get Sammy changed into her fancy dress. She's going to be two next week. Here's my little baby now walking and talking and I know it will soon be, "Dad, can I borrow the keys to the car?" My life seems to be accelerating. I thought publishing my book was somehow going to change my life. However, I'm still a nobody author who works for the government. I just don't know how I can fill in 822 forms and make banal pleasantries in the office coffee room for the next twenty years.

Normally on Saturday mornings I take Sammy to a parent and child sing-and-dance music program that's supposed to be good for developing minds. I do it to give Sarah a break, let her sleep in. There are twelve kids in the class, each with an accompanying parent. Eighty percent are dads. The reason for so many dads I believe is Katia, the former Russian ballet dancer turned dance instructor. Usually she prances around in a black unitard, often stretching before class. Most of the dads seem to arrive early to watch. Although I'm missing Katia's flexibility show this week, I'm very happy to have the day off from class. Dancing around with a scarf like a magic fairy for forty-five minutes is enough to make you right mental.

Sammy and I are playing with her stuffed bear, Mr. Honey, who's on a treacherous spelunking expedition in the closet after a harrowing trip to the top of Pillow Mountain, when Sarah finally emerges eons later from the bathroom, her makeup looking rather clownish. I've never understood why she applies so much lacquer and goo to her beautiful face on these festive occasions. "How do I look?" Sarah asks.

"You look beautiful, Mommy," Sammy says.

Sarah and I look at each other and share this moment which is heartbreakingly sweet because it is the first time Sammy has ever said that. "Oh, thank you, baby," says Sarah, picking up Sammy and swinging her around. "Don't you look just adorable?"

I marvel at them.

"And what do you think?" Sarah asks me.

"Like Sammy said, you look beautiful," I lie. She looks like a Tammy Faye Baker cross-dresser. Her eyelashes appear to have been dipped in motor oil.

We make our way to the church where we find Phil and his

groomsmen, Roy and Ross. Phil looks fantastic, beaming. We go about doing the multiple introductions to Phil and Zoe's respective families. Zoe's mother is French-Canadian and her father is Mexican, so the bride's side of the church is not big enough to hold them all.

Halfway through the ceremony, Sammy throws a fit and comes running up to me saying she needs her daddy. I hold her in my arms for the duration and by the time it's done, I'm sweating something fierce. I could use a drink. Sarah takes Sammy for a walk while I do the obligatory wedding photos. The reception and dinner are at Zoe's uncle's restaurant, a Mexican place. On arriving, we're greeted by a waiter carrying a tray of tall glasses of cold sangria. I snag one and greedily choke it down. The food and drink come at us, tidal wave after tidal wave. Polishing off my third drink to a mariachi serenade of "La Cucaracha," Sarah tells me to ease off the drink because tonight is an important night in our fertility schedule.

"But baby, this is Phil's wedding and I'm the best man," I plead with her.

"I still need you to function."

"Don't worry baby, I'll be a rock."

At 10 p.m., after much drink, food, speeches and dancing, Sarah takes Sammy, who is very overdue for sleep, back to the B&B. I stay and have a cigar and a gold tequila with Zoe's father. At 11:00, I realize I'd better get going. I make the rounds of the place, hugging strangers goodbye, many of them telling me how funny my speech was. Both Phil and Zoe give me a big warm hug. I'm lightheaded, giddy. Drunk, but not too drunk. And the thought of sex right now sends a wave of heat to my groin. Sarah baby, here I come.

To my surprise, the door of the B&B is locked. I ring the buzzer and wait. Nothing. I ring it again. Nothing. I have to take a piss. I knock and yell, "Helloooo!" Then through the glass square of the door, I see the little old man who runs the place coming down the hall. He lets me in and mumbles something in French that I don't understand, but assume to be that I don't need to yell, that people are sleeping.

"Yestankyougoodnigh," slurs from my mouth as I march up the stairs, thoughts of intercourse filling my mind. On the third set of steps leading to my door, I trip, falling up the stairs. Sarah emerges in the stairwell shushing me. "For God's sakes, be quiet, I just got her down twenty minutes ago. She was a nightmare. I had to rub her back to sleep. She's in our bed."

"Do you want me to transfer her?" I ask, rising to my feet.

"And risk waking her up? Hell no."

"What about love-making?"

"We'll do it in the bathroom," she says with an enthusiastic we-can-conquer-any-tough-problem zeal echoing in her voice.

"Jesus baby, I don't know, it's pretty tight in there."

Listening to Sammy softly wheezing on the bed, Sarah and I quietly disrobe in the bedroom like giddy high school kids. My cock is suddenly, to my delight and surprise, an iron bar. I follow Sarah into the bathroom and shut the door behind me. The wall is on an angle because we're in the attic of this old building and I can only stand fully upright if I'm in front of the sink or in the single-person shower. My cock is poking Sarah in her lower back. "I don't think this is going to work," I say.

"How about I sit on the toilet and put my legs up on the wall like this?" she suggests, getting into position.

I furrow my brow. Is this even possible? There's a tiny sink, the toilet next to it, and a shower with a door that only opens inwards because there's no space. In front of the toilet, there's a small window with an accompanying eight-inch ledge. Sarah's feet straddle either side of the window. I pull her one leg up as if it were a drawbridge and scoot in. With my butt resting on the window sill, ass cheeks pressed up against the window so I'm mooning the world, I reach over Sarah and grab hold of the toilet tank for support. She inches forward and we have contact. Despite being in this slightly uncomfortable sex pretzel, I'm loving it. There's something about the angle of penetration that seems to be working for both of us. Good news is I know that I'll be able to cum; bad news is I know it's going to be a while.

Twenty minutes later…

"My back's getting sore, can you hurry up?" Sarah groans.

I've talked about determinism before. What we think about and how we control that thinking is almost random at times for me. For whatever reason, maybe because my brain deems this to be a sexual emergency, I involuntarily flash to the bikini-clad sandy blonde from the cover of the *Sports Illustrated* swimsuit calendar that I stared at for four hours while I did my book signing. But then I think about Brian Mulroney. God almighty. My brain is doing a gestalt switch, back and forth between bikini blonde and Mulroney. I ask myself why but nothing comes, including Marvin.

"Colin, I love it, but my back is killing me. I'm going to have to stop soon," Sarah says with pain in her voice. I hear hooting and hollering from the street below and suspect that someone has noticed, as we called it in university when we pushed our bare asses against a dormitory window, the pressed ham. I soldier on. Mulroney, bikini, Mulroney, bikini, Mulroney, bikini, Mulroney, bikini… oh God. It's a gusher. I cum to an image of Mulroney's head on the body of one of the most beautiful women in the world.

I look out the window and sure enough there are three young men cheering, clapping, drinking. One of them gives me the thumbs up, while another spins around and drops his pants exposing his white buttocks to me. I smile and wave in acknowledgement of their approval. Moving into the bedroom, I note Sarah lying on the floor with her feet against the door, making sure that all of my drunken sperm stay deep inside her. I gingerly transfer Sammy to her portable crib, managing (thank heavens) not to wake her.

I lie down and I let sleep pull me deep into its loving arms.

Wolfgang AmADDeus

From: #The Refrigerator Committee
Date: 2009/04/20 AM 6:47:01 EDT
To: #FLOOR
Subject: The Abuse of "No Expiry"

To All Fifth-floor Employees:

This is a reminder that the refrigerator on this floor is for everyone to share. As everyone is well aware, every Friday afternoon a member of the Refrigerator Committee cleans out the
fridge. Any food items that are not clearly marked with a name
and an expiration date are tossed out in the trash. Some people
have condiments in the fridge that have been labelled "no
expiry." The "no expiry" tag was intended for such things as
mustard and hot sauce. However, since the "no expiry" tag has

come into effect, there has been rampant abuse. One Refrigerator Committee member found a container of yogourt that had
turned into a mossy green forest because someone had marked
"no expiry" across its lid. Clearly this kind of abuse must end.
Yogourt does go bad. Even ketchup goes bad.

From this Friday forward, ALL FOOD INCLUDING CONDI-
MENTS MUST HAVE AN EXPIRY DATE. Failure to comply will
result in the aforementioned disposal.

Thank you in advance for your cooperation.

–The Refrigerator Committee

Attached to the email is a *Far Side* cartoon, "When potato
salad goes bad." If this isn't silly enough, Barry has sent out
a floor-wide email about mandatory participation in next
month's Earth Day campaign: Operation Spring Clean. We're
all going to wander around outside the building and pick up
garbage. Lovely. I must say, I'd rather collect trash than sit in
here and die another day. I wonder how poor Carla's going to
handle this. Bruce has sent me an email stating that Wolfgang
will be reporting to work today. There had been a problem with
his security clearance, so his start date had been delayed for
three weeks.

Opening Internet Explorer, I navigate to the Stanzas website
where I can check to see how many copies of *The Cube People*
are sitting at the Sunshine Valley Mall location. Still five. No
sales in three weeks. I Google myself hoping to find a review
of my book. Nothing new. I check the weather and the CBC
headlines. After reading a story about a dog that called 911 to

save his owner, I log into the mainframe to start my day's work just as Carla comes in and takes several big glugs of hand sanitizer.

At 10:30, Bruce lightly raps his knuckles on my desk. "Hi, Colin, finally he's here. Let me introduce you to Wolfgang Peters, ta dah!" Bruce says, holding his hands out magician style.

Standing before me is a slightly fatter version of a young Peter Falk wearing a white shirt with a red plaid vest and a thin black tie. He looks as if he should be a bartender in Scotland. When I shake his hand, it's wet and clammy, toadish. Bruce asks me to run him through the log-in procedure and get him set up, make sure he has all the accesses he needs to get going.

Wolfgang and I sit down at his desk, Jackie's old spot, and surprisingly manage to log in on our first attempt. Thirty minutes in, as I'm explaining one of our reporting log procedures, Wolfgang's expression goes blank and he tilts his head up toward the ceiling. I look up to where he's looking and see nothing but office ceiling tiles. I look back at him. He's frozen, a statue.

"Wolfgang?" Nothing. "Wolfgang?" I repeat, waving my hand in front of his face. This seems to slightly arouse him back into a semi-conscious state.

"Hmmm yes," he says dreamily. I assume here that Wolfgang is having an ADD moment. I'm not sure what I should do. How long will his state (for a lack of a better word) last? I have no idea. Although he's no longer staring at the ceiling, he doesn't seem to be fully back with me as I continue to explain the log. It's only a quarter after eleven, but I suggest we break for an early lunch.

"Okay, that sounds fine," he drones as if he were under deep hypnosis. I need to get out of the office. I instinctively make my way to Phil's desk before I remember he's still on his month-long honeymoon in Hawaii. I decide to head over to Sunshine Valley. Crossing the street, I ponder some way to sabotage the plumbing in the handicapped washroom to render it permanently inoperable. Barry's need to justify the handicapped washroom has nothing to do with affirmative action, but rather with Barry having a nice private place to take a dump. I foresee myself having to babysit Wolfgang. I'm angry and it's only been thirty minutes.

On autopilot, I've wandered into Stanzas. I skim the titles on the "New and Hot" table. My book is absent, though the manager had put my extra copies there after my signing. I casually saunter over to the Science Fiction section. All five copies sit on the bottom shelf, their spines facing out. A lot of the other books have their covers facing out. I quickly rearrange the books so the cover of mine faces outwards. I grab three of the books and march them back to the "Hot" table and remove six copies of *The Gargoyle 2*, stashing these on the shelf below. Shameful I know. It's reverse shoplifting, but still thrilling and dirty. Pleased with my own handiwork, I continue on to the food court to get myself lunch.

Now seated next to the faux waterfall, I eat my sandwich as I gaze out upon the shoppers of Sunshine Valley. There's Freddy Fruitcake and the scooter lady in her bathrobe passing each other, as I'm quite sure they do several times daily. And here I am observing them, again. I'm the Jane Goodall of Sunshine Valley. When will it change? How many more years will I sit here? I could use a drink.

I envision myself dying, a sudden heart attack perhaps – what else? The headstone reads *Colin MacDonald, Sunshine Valley will never forget you. RIP*. It's softly raining and the staff of The Shawarma Pit are there, as well as Freddy Fruitcake, the old lady (but in a black bathrobe), the ladies from First Choice, the manager from Stanzas, all my MRC coworkers wearing bunny slippers, and a little crying Sammy who's asking her mom why her dad spent so much time at the mall. It's a humorous but horrifying image. I need to write a book that has the words "*New York Times* Bestseller" stamped across its cover. I need stickers: "Hugo Winner," "Sophie's Choice," "GG Winner," "Nebula Winner," "Oprah's Book Club."

Crossing back to my building, I dread the thought of having to sit with Wolfgang and coach him. My shoulders relax as I round the corner into my quad and see he hasn't returned from lunch. Then ZAP, as if I'd jabbed my finger into an electrical socket, I hear his voice from behind me: "Oh, Colin, great you're back, do you want to continue?" All my internal strings pull tight. I smile and say, "Whenever you're ready."

An hour later, Wolfgang freezes up again right in the middle of an explanation of file layouts. I tell him that I'm going to the washroom, not caring if he understands.

Looking at the walls of the handicapped washroom, I wish Crazy Larry were here with his sledgehammer. I stare into the mirror and think about my epitaph: *Here lies Colin MacDonald, dead by attrition.*

Hungry Hole

Chapter 18

Ryan answered the door. The man standing before him didn't look like a plumber. He looked more like Columbo, dressed in a trench coat and slacks.

The man looked down at his notebook, and then looked up at Ryan.

"Are you Mr. Ryan Smith?"

"Yes."

"I'm Detective Chris Farms," he announced, holding up a badge. "I'm investigating the disappearance of Barry Rodriguez."

"Don't know him," said Ryan, feeling sweat form across his brow.

"Here's his picture, do you mind taking a look?" he asked, holding up the photo.

"Nope, never seen him before," lied Ryan.

"Mr. Rodriguez was a plumber. Has a plumber come by your house in the last week or so?"

"No, there have been no plumbers here."

"Well the reason I'm asking you, Mr. Smith, is because Mr. Rodriguez always keeps a log of his jobs. He did a job last Tuesday only five blocks from here."

"Well did you check with them?"

"I did. Mr. Rodriguez went and fixed a toilet. Then he left. His next stop was here at 1:15."

"That's strange," said Ryan.

"Yes, it is, Mr. Smith, especially after you told me that you've had no plumbers come here. Why would Mr. Rodriguez have you down for," he pauses and looks down at his notebook, "a leaking basement pipe?"

"It was my wife. She must have called him."

"Oh, your wife, I see. Is she in?"

"No, she's at work. That's right, now that you mention it, the other day she did say something about getting a leaky pipe in the basement fixed."

"So you do remember a plumber coming here?"

"I wasn't here at the time. Gillian must have let him in."

"Can you give me your wife's number at work?"

"Ah, sure."

"Would you mind if I came in and took a look at the pipe he fixed?"

"Ah, no, follow me."

Detective Farms followed Ryan down into the basement.

* * *

When Ryan came back upstairs carrying the bloodied notebook, the doorbell rang again. He hid the notebook behind a vase in the hallway.

When Ryan opened the door, a big man with dirty jeans and shirt and a tool belt around his waist stood there.

"You must be the main course, I mean, you must be the plumber?"

"Leaking pipe?"

"Follow me, it's in the basement."

Earth Day: Operation Spring Clean

I've had a month of Wolfgang and my sanity is fractured. I grab the small stapler off Dan's desk and head into the handicapped washroom. After wrapping it up in a wad of paper towel, I drop it in the toilet, and then proceed to take the most satisfying dump of my life. I wipe using an excessive amount of tissue, then flush. My semi-mummified turd slowly circles the bowl waiting in vain for watery suction that never comes. The water rises to the lip of the seat. I know that this act of sabotage is passive-aggressive and immature. However, it's now my mission to never let Barry shit in here again. I wash my hands and head out to the elevator to join the rest of my section who are waiting outside for Earth Day: Operation Spring Clean.

Approximately twenty-five people are in Barry's section. They're all grouped around the large brown dumpster at the back of the building. Line's smoking and looks pissed off. Barry is there wearing his smiley-face tie and handing out garbage bags and rubber gloves, the kind that medical personnel use. Carla's decked out in a gas mask, goggles, and a one-piece white plastic suit with yellow rubber gloves. She's either ready for a biohazard recovery squad or a grow-op bust. Barry announces, holding up a bathroom scale, that there will be a prize given out for the most interesting item found and for the most garbage collected by weight.

"Yes, Colin, what is it?" asks Barry as he sees the puzzled look upon my face.

"Well, if I pick up a car battery and let's say Jill here picks up thirty pop cans, she'll have picked up more garbage but I'll still have the bigger weigh-in. See what I'm saying?" The crowd awaits Barry's response with an eager thirst to see him falter. Barry isn't all that popular; in fact, he's strongly disliked. He rubs his chin and ogles the scales. I'm not sure whether he's trying to understand what I've just told him or whether in fact he does understand and is trying to formulate a response that will not make himself look like an asshole.

His head cranes up and he says, "Good point, Colin. I guess we'll just have to eyeball then."

"How about recycling?" asks Jill.

"What about it?" fires back Barry with a thin tone of irritation.

"Well surely we aren't going to put recyclable materials such as pop bottles and cans in the same bag as garbage, are we?" asks Jill, her chipper Refrigerator Committee voice resounding in everyone's ears.

I can almost see Barry's mind twisting. He takes a deep breath and pauses. "That's why we're going to divide into two groups. Half will pick up trash and half will pick up recycling. As a matter of fact, find a partner and decide who's going to do trash and who's going to do recycling."

People quickly head twist, frantically looking for the least painful coupling option available. Before I can get away,

Wolfgang's at my side. "Howdy partner, do you want to be the garbage guy or the recycling guy?" he asks me happily.

"I don't care," I tell him.

"Okay, you're garbage then," he says with a chuckle.

We all fan out, two by two, moving through the maze of cars in the parking lot behind our building, strolling toward the grassy bike path. I pick up a cigarette butt (probably Line's) and immediately have a desire to go out and buy a pack of smokes. We make our way over to the other side of the bike path. A ten-foot fence and a small hill lead down to the Transitway, where only city buses are allowed to travel. Wolfgang and I are walking along the fence when he spots a woman's red high-heeled shoe lying in the grass on the other side. "It's mine, it's mine," he squeaks excitedly. Before I can talk him out of such insanity, I watch his pudgy little hedgehog frame scramble up the fence, presumably in an attempt to win Barry's coveted most-interesting-piece-of-garbage prize. He's going to kill himself I think. Good. At the top he looks rather worried, straddling the fence as if he were sitting on a giant rodeo bull, the gate about to open. As he swings his other leg over I hear the sound of ripping fabric. He's managed to snag one pant leg on a wire and is flailing about, desperately trying to free himself.

"Help Colin!" he screams, but it's too late. He loses his grip trying to unhook himself. He falls with one pant leg still firmly attached to the fence. His pants rip apart at the seam of his crotch. The result of such action cartwheels Wolfgang down the side of the fence where he lands with a scream and a mighty thud. Several people come running over, joining me. We watch Wolfgang rolling around on the ground, clutching his ankle.

"Are you all right?" I ask as the pant leg flutters in the wind above us, a windsock or perhaps a new flag to represent Earth Day.

"I think I might have broken it," he whines.

"Well at least you got the shoe," I say, trying to make him feel better. With those words and his eye still firmly on the prize, he bolts up and scours around for it. He sees it and reaches out for it. He freezes just before he's about to grab it. His hand recoils. "There's something inside it," he whimpers. "I think it's a finger."

I turn to Barry, who has wandered over. "Well," I say smiling, "I think we've found our winner."

I tell Wolfgang not to touch it and then call 911 on my cell to notify them of our gruesome little discovery. Grabbing hold of the fence, Wolfgang manages to pull himself to a standing position on his one good leg, exposing half of his light blue briefs and his bare leg with a watermelon-sized ankle. Staring at the finger within the shoe, Wolfgang announces he's going to be sick. This announcement is immediately followed by projectile vomit, followed by a chorus of *ewws* from the crowd.

The police show up and immediately cut a large hole in the fence to free Wolfgang and to get in to examine "the finger." Soon four more police cruisers and a media van descend upon our environmental merrymaking. The whole back parking lot is declared a crime scene and yellow police tape is put up to cordon off the area. All the garbage and recycling that we've collected is seized as evidence. They take statements from Wolfgang, Barry and me, as well as a few others who saw Wolfgang's accident.

They call an ambulance for Wolfgang. I ask if I can tag along. Wolfgang seems touched that I would stay with him until he finds out that I really only want a ride because I've got to go to the ultrasound clinic which is only a few blocks away from the hospital. I call Sarah and tell her not to bother picking me up, that I'll meet her there. After the wedding in Montreal, Sarah became pregnant. She's just past six weeks, so we have an appointment to see if everything looks right with the fetal pole, which is the size of a grain of rice. Just before the door to the ambulance shuts, Wolfgang asks Barry, who is still standing outside looking rather dazed, what does he get for a prize?

"A free month in the water cooler club," answers Barry cheerfully. Wolfgang seems surprisingly happy with that. Maybe he hit his head. A month in the water cooler club is worth five dollars.

I give Wolfgang my cell number and tell him to give me a ring if he needs a pick-up later. Yeah the guy drives me nuts, but it's not really his fault, he has ADD. The ultrasound clinic is located on the fifth floor of a busy building that strangely has only one tiny elevator. There is a six-person line to ride up, which is the max it can hold. I have to wait until it comes back a second time. When I open the door to the ultrasound office, I see Sammy playing with Mr. Honey on a little kid's table in the corner of the large waiting room. She doesn't see me come in, so I quietly make my way over to Sarah, who is catching up on the latest fashion news in *Cosmo*, and take a seat beside her. "Hi," I whisper softly.

"Hi there," she says. We both look over at Sammy who seems to be lost in a world of make-believe.

"She's so cute," I say. "I can't believe she's ours."

"Can you believe we're going to have another one?"

"No, it's crazy." I'm never going to be able to quit my job, I think.

Sammy looks over and sees me. She runs, arms wide, screaming "Daaaaadddddyyy!" I bend down to swoop her up. We squeeze each other tightly. You can't buy this love, but I can't keep going to work to pay for it. "Mommy has a baby in her tummy," Sammy says, patting her own tummy.

"That's right, we're going to see the baby. But right now the baby is very small."

"Tiny one?" Sammy asks or says, for I'm not sure if it's a question or merely a statement.

"It's small now, but it's going to get big like you."

One of the ultrasound technicians calls us in. The room is dark and probably creepy if you're two years old. Sammy's clutching Mr. Honey tightly. Sarah lies back on the table, lifts her shirt and lowers her pants to expose her lower abdomen. The technician squirts a translucent blue gel on Sarah's belly. "What doing?" asks Sammy.

"They put that on so the machine can see the baby," I say, not really understanding what the blue gel does either, but I presume my guess must be close.

"Actually, in your case, Mr. MacDonald," says the technician, "it's to see the babies."

"Pardon?" Did I hear that right?

"Babies. See here," she says, pointing to the two dots on the screen. "You and your wife are going to have twins."

Hungry Hole

Chapter 20

Ryan lay fully dressed, shoes still on, atop the neatly made bed. He imagined lying in a coffin. He could hear it all the way up here, breathing. It was beckoning him. He could feel its hunger in his bones, in his heart. Every once in a while he thought he heard Gillian call out to him.

DING DONG.

Ryan got up and went to the window. Two cop cars were parked on the street. He knew what he had to do. He walked downstairs, down the hallway to the basement door. He went down the stairs and stood at the edge of the hole.

He jumped.

Nine months later...

Cube Squared

Sarah threw up every day for six months straight before her appetite returned. During this period, we purchased a three-bedroom house and a minivan in order to accommodate our expanding brood, which we found out was to include a baby girl and baby boy. For a moment I thought we should name the babies Brian and Sandy after Brian Mulroney and the sandy blonde *Sports Illustrated* girl, but then thought better of it. I suggested Kurt for the boy after Kurt Vonnegut. Also my publisher is Kurt. Sarah went with it. She wanted Alexandra for a girl and I happily agreed. But we call her Alex. Sounds like we have three boys: Sammy, Kurt and Alex. Sarah had a C-section. Three weeks later, her incision became infected and she ended back up in the hospital for two days. Otherwise, it's been smooth; no baby blues this time around. My mother's been very helpful: cleaning our house, doing laundry, paying extra attention to Sammy to help her adjust now that she has to share the limelight.

I'm back in the office after being away for almost eight

weeks. A Kafka character would look joyful compared to me. I love my kids too much to commit suicide, but I'm only an inch away from keeping a bottle in my desk drawer. There are over a thousand emails to go through. I spend a good part of the morning just deleting garbage Bruce has sent me, mostly statistical comparisons between programs. Dan waltzes in at quarter after eleven expressing his great joy at having me back; apparently Bruce has been riding his ass about everything. Dan was off last Thursday and Friday because of all the stress Bruce has been putting him under. Wasting no time in bringing me up to speed, Dan spends thirty minutes providing me with an overview of his sufferings of the past eight weeks. I'm tempted to share some of mine, but Phil shows up to announce it's time to get the fuck out of Dodge. Dan realizes instantly that the conversation, or should I say his monologue, is now over. Phil doesn't understand how I put up with it; I'm not sure I understand either.

Biting into my shawarma sandwich, my mouth explodes in flavours of garlic, succulent chicken, pickled turnip, onion and hot peppers. I haven't had a shawarma in over a month. I realize that aside from Phil's company, this is the only thing I've missed about work, if you could call this "work." After we eat we go to Stanzas and check on my book. There are now only four copies. In all probability somebody I know bought one, though I hold out hope it was a stranger. Phil does the honours and rearranges the books so my cover faces outwards. He's great.

As I'm crossing the street back to work, I'm dizzy. I press my fingers to my neck desperately searching for a pulse. I'm having an anxiety attack. I haven't had one in a good long while and this one takes me by surprise. Phil's talking a mile a minute and doesn't seem to notice I'm in distress, for which I'm glad because I'm hoping that this wave of panic will soon pass. It thankfully does as we wait for the elevator.

Hacking my way through the forest of emails, I come across a bizarre one. It's from me, dated last week. I don't have a smart phone, nor was I in the office, so I'm not sure how this is possible unless somebody logged onto my computer with my user ID and password – but I don't think that is possible. Even if they did, who would send this and why?

From: Colin MacDonald
Date: 2010/04/02 PM 1:22:02 EDT
To: Colin MacDonald
Subject: Wasn't it always going to happen this way?

Dear Colin:

Be on the lookout for a package in the mail.

Your Loving Uncle Buck

My loving Uncle Buck? I swivel in my chair, squinting into the light of Dan's SunSquare Plus.

"Can you turn that goddamn thing off? It's been on for the last half an hour."

"Will do, Colin. Gotta keep fighting the depression," he says, flicking it off.

"Listen, did you see anyone use my computer last week?" I say gruffly.

"No, no one that I know of, but as I told you I wasn't here Thursday or Friday."

"Wolfgang, did you see anybody using my machine last week?"

Spinning around, Wolfgang shakes his head. I look over at Carla and she shakes her head in anticipation of the question.

"Strange," I say.

"What is it?" asks Dan.

I smell burnt toast. Am I about to have a seizure? Just as I finish saying, "Does anyone smell that?" the fire alarm sounds. Normally people wouldn't do anything, but living in a post-Crazy-Larry world, coupled with the odour of something possibly ablaze, people start hustling toward the fire exits at a good clip. The smell of smoke is strong in the stairwell and I wonder if going down is the best idea, but the smell dissipates after passing the fourth floor. We all gather outside as the fire trucks come roaring up. Speaking with others, it turns out that there is indeed a fire on the fourth floor, and it's widely suspected somebody named James Morgan had a toaster oven in his cubicle and somehow it overloaded the circuit, setting his cubicle afire. I mill about for thirty minutes and realize it's almost time for me to go home anyway. I find Bruce and tell him I'm splitting, just in case somebody plans on doing a head count. I wouldn't want anyone looking for my charred corpse.

My mother's sitting on the couch knitting and watching *The Young and the Restless* when I walk in. "Shhhh, not too loud, the twins are sleeping," she says, raising an index finger to her lips. The TV seems to be at regular listening volume, so I find her statement rather puzzling. And since when does my mother knit?

"Where are Sarah and Sammy?"

"Uh, they went to get groceries. Victor Newman is about to

be poisoned."

"That's nice Mom. I'm going to go down to my writing room." She nods ever so slightly, so engrossed in her show that I wonder if she really knows that I've come home, or whether she's on autopilot? Have you ever driven home and not known how you got there? The brain is a marvellous thing.

As soon as I log on to my computer, I hear the cry of one of the twins over the baby monitor. Back upstairs I go. Sarah bursts through the front door saddled down with a zillion bags of groceries. Sammy has a plastic bag, too. By the strain on her little face it appears to weigh more than she does. Sarah looks haggard. As I help Sarah with the bounty, both babies wail out and my mother is screeching at the TV, "Don't drink it, Victor! Don't drink it, Victor. It's poison, Victor! Poison!"

It's about 11:30, just after I've fallen asleep. Sammy woke up having peed the bed, so I do the whole sheet-changing business and get back to sleep. Maybe an hour later, the twins wake up. So now it's two in the morning and I've just helped Sarah give the twins a feed and I've changed their diapers. But for whatever reason, they're not settling down. I don't want them to wake up Sammy. Sarah looks as if she hasn't slept in eons. I put the twins into their bucket car seats and take them for a little drive. They both fall back to sleep after fifteen minutes, but I continue to drive for another fifteen, just to make sure they're out cold. Carrying them back inside, I dare not traverse the creaky stairs for fear of waking up anyone and setting off a chain reaction. Still in their car seats with blankets snuggled around each, I place them on the floor of the living room and go about fashioning myself a bed out of couch cushions and an itchy red and purple afghan. I close my eyes and I'm out.

I dream of shoving body parts down toilets and having sex with Angelina Jolie. As I'm fucking her, all six of her kids are watching. She doesn't seem to notice; she's just wild. Sarah and I haven't had sex in several months. It's difficult to maintain a regular sex life through this baby stage of our lives. We just need to ride this wave out. At least that's what I keep telling myself.

I awake as the sun is climbing out of bed. The sky looks like a copy of the afghan which I'm clutching onto for dear life because I'm freezing and have the biggest aching boner of my life. Kurt and Alex are still sleeping. The house is quiet. I grab Marvin and decide to deal with him promptly while fresh visions of Angelina's breasts still dance in my head. I stroke quietly and quickly. Oh Angie, you bad girl. Oh you dirty, dirty girl. Oh... Alex lets out a small cry. She's stirring. I try and stay focused. Come on Marvin, don't let me down. "Waaaaannnn," cries Alex, then seconds later Kurt lets out a howl. Fuck. It's not working. I can't finish. Pulling up my boxers, the elastic band of my underwear snaps Marvin back, choking him into wilting submission. I get them out of their car seats and bring them up to Sarah for breastfeeding. Sammy awakes and asks for juice and if she can watch her *Wiggles* DVD. I go about accommodating these requests. I make some breakfast for everyone and prepare to go to work on three hours of sleep.

Two months later...

Quitting Time

From: Central Services
Date: 2010/06/04 AM 8:01:00 EDT
To: Colin MacDonald
Subject: Removal of Hazardous Materials

As you are aware, all items deemed to be a possible fire hazard have been removed from the building. You were found to have an item(s) in your cubicle that was considered to be dangerous. We have removed your `coffee maker` from your workstation. You may pick it up at the security desk on the ground floor when exiting the building.

Thank you for your understanding and cooperation in this important matter.

—Central Services

My coffee maker has been seized. After the toaster-oven fire, there was an official sweep. A crackdown is what Barry called it. Government safety inspectors went from cubicle to cubicle, searching for whatever management deemed to be any possible fire hazard. So if you had anything – coffee warmer, electric pencil sharpener, CD player, etc. – it was gonzo. Even Dan's SunSquare Plus was removed. I can't say that I'm too sad about that. He's gone to the union and is fighting to get it returned. Without my coffee maker, I'm depressed (maybe I could use a little SunSquare). The only joy I had in my cubicle has been stripped away. I log onto the Stanzas website and check how many copies of my book are at the Sunshine Valley Mall location: still four. "Hey MacDonald," yells Dan from behind me, "you sent me two specs to review, but they're exactly the same. Which one do you want me to review?"

"Are they exactly the same?" I fire back, realizing I must have accidently attached my document twice.

"Yeah, I looked really closely at them and they're identical, even checked the date and time stamp on them and they're the same."

I have a missile-launcher mouth jammed with fresh cut, grade-A go-fuck-yourself sarcasm and it's ready to fire right at Dan's head, but what comes out instead is a polite, "Then I would just do the first one."

"Okay, thanks buddy," he says, happy to carry on.

I turn back to my screen, close my eyes and rub my temples. I repeat to myself, I won't kill Dan, I won't kill Dan, I won't kill Dan. BEEP, chimes my machine. I have an email. I Alt-Tab over. There's a message from Line that a package for me has arrived. As I approach Line, I spot a manila parcel sitting on her desk. The sender's name in black marker in the upper left-hand corner reads "U. Buck" and has my previous home address. "Do I need to sign for it or anything?" I ask Line.

"No, no, just take it off my desk and have a nice day," she says, continuing to type away without bothering to make eye contact. It's about the same size and weight as a shoebox containing an explosive device – at least that is what my paranoid imagination surmises. How much does dynamite weigh anyway? U. Buck? Uncle Buck. What did the email say, be on the lookout for a package in the mail? I wonder if Phil is playing some sort of an elaborate practical joke. Nervously, I rip open the paper at one end and inspect the contents. There appears to be more paper, Christmas wrapping paper with little Santa Clauses on it. Written atop the present is an envelope which reads, "Open the letter and gift in a private place," in the same black marker and handwriting. Could it be Crazy Larry? Maybe it's a nail bomb? He wants to make sure he kills just me and nobody else. Jesus. Now I'm not sure what to do. Maybe I should go get Phil? The Santas look like the Coca-Cola Santa, a Norman Rockwell Santa. In Santa I trust. I go to the handicapped washroom and lock the door behind me. I sit down and open the letter.

Dear Colin:

First let me apologize for having deceived you. I always enjoyed our conversations and considered you a good worker and a dear friend. I took advantage of your good nature and used you to further my own gain. For this I'm terribly sorry; however, I will not apologize for the theft. Over the years, I saw so much rampant abuse of government dollars that I figured it was time for my share. Rest assured the money is going to a noble cause.

For all the inconvenience and suffering that the RCMP and/or police have put you through, please consider this gift as a small restitution for my actions. Try not to let that good conscience of yours get the better of you.

Warmest regards, Peter Cann

PS: Congratulations on the publication of *The Cube People*. It's a wonderful book.

I tear into the Christmas wrapping and discover three hardback copies of Stephen King's *Nightmares and Dreamscapes*. Peter and I have discussed King's work in the past; however, I was hoping he would have sent me some money. I open the cover of the first book and sure enough, Peter has removed the guts of the book, leaving only the tiniest edge of paper. The paper's been replaced with three stacks of one hundred dollar bills. Same for the other books. I do a quick count and there is approximately $300,000. "Holy shit," I whisper. I rewrap the books, bring them to my desk and put them in my backpack. I pretend to do work, but my mind is in fantasy land, sipping tropical drinks with little umbrellas underneath palm trees on the beach. Should I give the money to the RCMP? Maybe I should just give them the note and copies of another book, and keep the money? This may be my only chance to get out of this place. My phone rings. "Hello," I say.
"Colin?"
"Yes."
"It's Sarah."
"Yes, hi, how are you?"
"Are you okay, you sound strange?"

"No, just busy here at work."

"Can you pick up milk on the way home?"

"Sure thing." After I get off the phone, I'm hot and my face feels flushed. I can hear Dan cutting his toenails. I pick up my knapsack and toss in my Shaggy and Scooby Doo action figures, my picture of Sarah and the kids, and a Pollockesque drawing that Sammy has done for me. As I pass by the handicapped washroom, I stop. I go in and lock the door. I turn off the water to the tank and flush the toilet, emptying the tank dry. I remove the tank's lid. While balancing with one foot on the toilet seat, I use my other to kick the plastic innards of the tank into smithereens. As I replace the lid, I'm struck by a sense of levity. All my flesh is coursing with life and when I breathe, I have new lungs. In a state of euphoria, I leave the washroom and make my way down the corridor.

There's Barry, sitting at his desk, warming himself by the glow of his monitor. Today he's wearing a tie with yellow rubber ducks on it. "Barry," I say, leaning into his office, hanging on the doorframe.

He looks up smiling, "Yes, Colin, what can I do for you?"

"I quit."

"Oh," he says, looking confused, like a waiter has brought him the wrong food.

"I've got to go now, but I'll be in touch in the next few days." I walk away and half-expect him to chase me down the hall, begging me to stay, but he doesn't. As I step on the elevator, a man and woman are already on, engaged in a conversation about applying for a competition. The woman seems annoyed by his banal banter and I wouldn't be surprised if she suddenly punched him in the nose. Within the thirty seconds it takes me to walk to the elevator, I've become an outsider. These are not my people anymore. I never have to make small talk again;

I never need to be annoyed. My days in the cube are officially over.

BING. The elevator doors open. I'm free.

Hungry Hole

Chapter 21

Ryan screamed as he fell. The air rushed around him. His body was tense, bracing itself for the impact that he assumed would come at any second. No impact came. He kept twirling and twisting in the darkness. He could no longer see the light coming from his basement's naked bulbs. There was just darkness and the whistling of wind in his ears. He expected the tentacle to grab him, but it didn't. Just falling, darkness. After a while, his body relaxed. He began to play in the air, twisting this way and that, rolling, flipping. The sound of the rushing air seemed to dissipate. Ryan was floating in space.

A flash of light whizzed by. Then another. Then another. They kept coming, but this succession of comet streaks eventually began to slow. They were windows. He tried to see what was inside, but he couldn't make it out. They continued to slow. He saw faces. People. Office workers. The windows slowed like an elevator. Ryan stood in a glass elevator. It came to a stop. The doors opened.

"Ryan, this is your floor," said the blonde woman to his left. He didn't understand what was happening. He recognized her. This was his old office building. He stepped out into the hallway. People rushed about him. He walked down the hall and through his company's glass door. As he walked, people kept tapping him on the shoulder, saying things like "Good luck," and "We're going to miss you around here." He continued to walk to his cubicle and sat down on his chair. Had he been dreaming? He touched the desk. He tapped on it. Solid. Real. What had he been thinking about? He couldn't remember. The phone rang. He picked it up.

"Hello?"

"Hi honey, how was your goodbye lunch?"

"Gillian?"

"Yeah silly, it's me. How was your goodbye lunch?"

"Goodbye lunch?"

"Listen, I'm picking you up right after work at four and we're going straight over to look at the house with the real-estate agent, okay?"

"Okay," Ryan said.

"Bye."

"Bye."

* * *

When Ryan climbed into the car, he looked at Gillian as if she were a ghost. He reached over and touched her face.

"What are you doing?" she asked.

"Just making sure you're real."

"Did you smoke dope at lunch?"

"No."

She looked at him. Ryan smiled back. "You sure?" she asked.

"Positive. Let's go."

* * *

The house seemed so familiar to Ryan, like a childhood home.

"So, Gillian here tells me that you quit your office job to

become a writer. Quite a big move. That's a gutsy thing to do. What kind of stuff do you write?" asked the agent.

"I write horror books," said Ryan.

"Really, just like Stephen King?"

"Just like Stephen King," said Ryan, wandering down the hall. He came to a door. He opened it. There were steps leading down.

"It's a little creepy, but I'm sure a writer like yourself will love it," said the agent from behind him.

Ryan flicked on the light and managed to hit his head on a cross beam on the way down. "You okay?" asked the agent.

"I'm okay," assured Ryan, rubbing his forehead.

Two bare light bulbs illuminated old wooden shelves atop flaking white walls. Behind the paint, sporadically exposed, was the rust-coloured underbelly of the foundation. It looked like the skin of a scab-ridden burn victim. Gillian came down the stairs. "Jesus, an *Amityville-Horror*-serial-killer-pit-of-hell down here," she said.

"Great for cold storage," said the agent.

"You could put your pickles and wine down here," said Ryan. As he said that, something flashed in front of his eyes.

"You okay honey?" Gillian asked.

"No, I mean yes, I think I'm just having a déjà vu," said Ryan.

Gillian turned to the agent. "Ryan suffers from epilepsy. Sometimes this is how it starts before a seizure hits."

"No, Gillian, I'm fine," said Ryan, as his body suddenly tightened and contorted and he fell to the ground and began to convulse.

* * *

"Just give me a minute," said Ryan, sitting on the bottom step of the basement stairs.

"Is he going to be okay?" asked the agent.

"He'll be fine," said Gillian.

"I think we should take it," said Ryan.

"What?" asked Gillian.

"The house, I think we should take it."

"Maybe you want to think about it?" suggested the agent.

"No, I feel the book in me coming out, this is the place."

"The book coming out?" questioned Gillian.

"I feel that I could write in this house. The seizure, it was a sign I think. What do you think of the house?"

"Well, except for this basement, it's great."

"Then we should put in an offer," said Ryan, smiling.

* * *

Ryan managed to hit the goddamn beam, *again*, on his way down to the cellar.

"Fuck," said Ryan.

"You okay honey?" asked a snickering voice that came from the top of the stairs.

"Remind me to..." he said but stopped. He turned and ran back up the stairs. Dean and Marsha were sitting on the floor. Ryan took the joint from Marsha's offering hand.

"I have an idea for a book," said Ryan, then he took a drag. He exhaled and they all listened as he told it.

The Smile of a Million Smiles

I'm in the garage staring at the stacks of money on my work-bench. Should I give it back? Three hundred thousand could buy me three, four, maybe even five years of writing. Surely in that time I could write the bestseller. I would need one to stay away from my day job permanently. It would buy me a shot. How many people are handed a chance like this? Is this fate? Could this have happened any other way? The door to the house opens and Sarah walks in yelling my name. I turn to her and say, "Hi honey."

"I've been looking all over for you, and..." She sees the money.

"What's that?"

"Three hundred thousand dollars," I answer.

"Where did you get it?"

"Peter Cann sent it to me."

"Have you called the police yet?"

"No."

"Why not? You can't keep it."

"Whoa there, Miss Conscientious, let's just take a second to think about this, shall we?"

"What's there to think about? If you get caught you'll go to jail. You have to give it back, Colin."

"Can you hear me out for one second?"

"No."

"Give me one chance at a sales pitch."

"Fine, pitch away," she says.

"This is my dream. I can have the time to write, I mean *really* write. No cubicles, no lines of code to change, no interruptions. I'll have peace and quiet. I can't listen to Dan drone on for the next twenty years about his failing body. I can't stand the smell of hand sanitizer in the morning. I can't deal with filling in my goddamn timesheet. Do you understand what I'm saying here? I'll be able to spend more time with the kids, with you. This is my chance. I don't want to end up a miserable failure. I don't want to be my father."

"Listen, Colin, I don't know what makes you think you're so special, but everybody goes to work. Everybody fills in their timesheet. Most people don't like it, but they do it just the same. That's just part of life. If you want to be a writer, then write. Real writers find the time. Taking this money, it's cheating. Besides, softness never made good art. You're the one who told me that. If you only have thirty minutes a day to write, then you'll write like it means something when you do write. It might not be any good, but the passion will be behind it. People will feel that. You need to give the money back. And don't worry, you're not your father."

I look at the towers of bills and imagine a world without fluorescent lighting.

Standing adjacent to the stage, I can see Sarah, the kids, and my mother sitting in the studio audience. They've pinned a cordless microphone to my shirt and have done a sound check. I'm nervous. My palms are rivers of sweat. I remember what Sarah told me: "People are here to see you. They want to see you, want to hear what you have to say. You're likeable, remember that."

She's speaking from her couch about her website and where you can go to find out more information. She says, "And when we return from our break, we'll be speaking with Colin Mac-Donald, author of *The Cube People*. It's one of my favourite books of the year, and it's soon to be a major motion picture directed by David Cronenberg. So please stay with us." The crowd applauds. The woman standing next to me with a clipboard and small headset motions for me to go out, to take my place on the stage. She rises off the couch and extends her hand. I feel as though I should drop to one knee and kiss her hand, but I don't. I grab it and she leans in and gives me a peck on the cheek and softly into my ear whispers, "Welcome." I take a seat on the couch next to her. She picks up my book and places it on her lap. She caresses it softly as if it were a cat. We do another sound check and we're set.

"Welcome back," she says, smiling at the camera. Her teeth are perfectly white, no traces of tea or coffee, but pure white, like printer paper, as if they're waiting for words to be typed upon them. Her mouth is a series of white pages bound elegantly by upper and lower lip covers, just waiting for that oval kiss, that sticker that says *Buy me*. I know now that I'll never need Peter Cann's money. I'm happy I decided to hand it over to the police, but at the time I felt as if I were a trapeze artist and somebody had just taken away the safety net. I didn't know it was going to turn out this way.

Her smile is the smile of a million smiles and when she asks me how I am, I tell her without any reservation or hesitation: "Fabulous."

BEEP BEEP BEEP... There's Marcus Jackson in the audience, clapping his hands together. Although I've never met him, I know it's him. Every time he brings his hands together they BEEP.

BEEP BEEP BEEP BEEP BEEP...

I hit the alarm clock off. Sarah rolls over, taking most of the duvet with her. Funny how your mind can play tricks on you. Do you really have any control over what you think? Was it always going to happen this way?

When I'd brought Peter Cann's gift of stolen money home, fear had danced in my heart. The image of me in an orange jumpsuit, Sarah bringing the kids to see their inmate father, flashed before my eyes. I went into work the next day and told Barry I'd been kidding. He'd said with a chuckle, "Thought you were." It's a good thing I did, because the next week, Kurt Jackson called me. He'd finished reading over *Hungry Hole* and told me he couldn't publish it. He said it wasn't strong enough, not nearly as good as *The Cube People*. Sarah had tried to be comforting. "Well, you know what Colin, whatever happens in your life, at least you managed to get published." I understood what she was trying to say, but her words felt like failure. I got a sinking feeling in my gut, a ball of wet clay. I've had that feeling in my stomach for two weeks now.

Just as I'm heading out the door to go to work, Sarah yells out for me not to forget my lunch. She comes running down the hall with a piece of Tupperware containing spaghetti leftovers, my name and expiry date written in ballpoint across a piece of masking tape on the lid. "Thanks," I say, kissing her lightly on the cheek.

I walk to the bus stop and wait. The sky is grey. When the bus arrives, I manage to get one of the last seats near the back. I softly drum the plastic lid of my lunch. I could be home, writing, if I'd only kept the money. I remind myself that good art doesn't come from cushiness. I could do with a few toss cushions though.

Glancing to my right I see a young man reading a book. Then I realize it's not just a book. A complete stranger is reading my book. *My book.* I don't make any sudden movements, like I've discovered some rare exotic bird and I don't want to scare it away. I observe him reading for several stops; he's got short-cropped hair, glasses, maybe twenty-five, neatly dressed. Maybe a university student? He seems fixated, intense. I'm filled with wonder and awe. He flips a page. "Excuse me," I say.

"Yes?" he answers sitting up straighter in his seat, pushing his glasses higher up his nose.

"I just wanted to know what you thought of your book. Are you enjoying it?"

"This?" he says, turning it over in his hands. "Yeah, I love it. One of the best books I've read in a while. Have you heard of it or something? I think the guy who wrote it is local."

"Yeah, I was thinking of getting a copy."

"You should, worth it," he says, and then goes back to reading.

Suddenly I realize I've missed my stop. I DING the bell and get off. As I walk back the ten blocks to work, I can't stop smiling: *one of the best books I've read in a while.*

When I get off the elevator, the air on my floor seems pungently stale. After I manage to cram my lunch into the overcrowded refrigerator, I make my way to my cubicle and log on to my machine. Fastened to the fabric wall of my cube, the photograph of Sarah and our three children stares at me.

The knot in my stomach seems to have relaxed, albeit ever so slightly.

I open Word and begin to type a new story:

The monster had him by the throat, but he wasn't afraid. He knew now that it wouldn't kill him.

Acknowledgements

I thank the Ontario Arts Council and the Canada Council for the Arts for their generous financial support during the time that I wrote this book.

Jeffrey Hodgson, Shelley Little, Tim MacIntosh, Ross Buskard, George Sneyd, Brenna MacNeil, Nicole Hillmer, Ken Sproule, Maria Wing, Cindy Christie, Graham O'Neil, Jules and Christopher Hilliker, Mark Saikaley, Marc-Andre Pigeon, Tom Macdonald and Don Mounteer, thank you all for reading.

For your support, thanks to: James and Megan Cantellow, Bill Rogers, Ben and Allison Lones, Bryan Gardner, Celine Dore, Claire McLaughlin, Barb Harris, Jennifer Stone, Colette Gignac, David Pringle, Henry Scott Smith, Sarah Bristow, Jason Mutch, Jen Baker, John Francis, Jean-Pierre Verreault, Brian Stoneman, Kathy and Scott Cowan, Kate and Shawn Charland, Kevin Ready, Neal Gillett, Rob White, Chris Sherlock, Jeanie Hicks, Luke Sneyd, Mike Hillmer, Christine Woodrow, Josiane St-Louis, Finlay MacLennan, Joanne Lee, Bob Kidman, Jeremy Galda, Terrie Osborne, Nona Ioan, Anita Comeau,

Juliette Lavoie-Goguen, James Wong, Sharon Pickles, Kelly Gillingham, Luciano Oliveira, Lynda McGahey, Pat Langhan, Rod Myers, Rohin Lakhani, Will Jan, David Schumann, Jesse Vallier, Phil Lee, Gina Cook, Eric Dumville, Dorothy Camire, Rob and Sonya Read, Peter McColgan, Kim Davison, and all my other friends in APD and DISA.

To my mother and talented photographer, Judith Gustafsson, thank you for all that you do. To my mother-in-law Susan Carr (who is very much unlike the mother-in-law in this book) thanks for all your love and support. To Lona Leiren and in loving memory of my father-in-law Russell Carr who passed away last year, bless you both. The Davis and Gustafsson teams, along with the extended Carr family – Ashley, Sarah and Kyle, much gratitude.

My succinct and unquestionably sane publisher, Silas White: thank you.

My beautiful wife, Marty, I love you as much as the day I met you.

And finally my kids, Molly and Henry, to whom this book is dedicated, you are the reasons I get out of bed (literally) and I love you with all my heart.